JOURNEYS

a short novel

-oOo-

Jane Street

Text copyright © 2013 Jane Street
All Rights Reserved

Cover design and illustration by Mat Street

Pilotshouse Publishing
www.pilotshouse.co.uk

ISBN 978-1-304-38117-0

Contents

JOURNEYS	1
Chapter 2	28
Chapter 3	34
Chapter 4	39
Chapter 5	47
Chapter 6	52
Chapter 7	67
Chapter 8	76
Chapter 9	82
Chapter 10	86

JOURNEYS

"I ought to be in bed, you know." The tone was brisk, almost reproving.

Iris's duster fluttered to a halt half-way along the mantelpiece. "But Jo, dear," the duster twitched, "you said you wanted to die with your boots on."

"Never mind what I said. Get me out of this chair."

"If you're quite sure." She had an idea. "Wait there a minute and I'll make you a hottie."

"Whatever for?"

She left the duster lying beside the clock and hurried into the kitchen. The bed would need airing. Josephine hadn't moved from her wing chair for days as far as she knew, not since she had announced that she was dying and that she intended to die there. After the second day she had stopped taking food, and would have refused even the sips of water Iris had offered her but for her insistence. For almost all of that time she had not spoken, and often Iris had been uncertain as to whether she was awake or asleep with her eyes open, if such a thing were possible.

"Oh, come on kettle, boil! Boil!" Kettles always seemed to come to the boil more rapidly for Josephine (not that she boiled that many) giving Iris sometimes to wonder whether she was blessed with special powers. Clocks and watches kept time for her and pearls regained their lustre, whereas for Iris such inanimate objects displayed all the perverseness for which they are justly celebrated, exhibiting a degree of animation, of animosity even, towards her intentions for them as to seem to give them an animus of their own. Nor was it only inanimate objects which bowed to Josephine's will: people and animals, plants too, responded in a noticeably positive way, and Iris was, therefore, more than a little surprised that Josephine, having stated that she was about to die (which she had, typically, made to sound a very positive act) was still alive, and that the process was taking as long as it was. In fact, now that she was speaking again, Josephine did not appear to be any nearer to death than she had been a week ago, and she hadn't seemed to be anywhere near it then.

The kettle boiled. She added some cold water to it so as not to rot the rubber, before laying the hot-water bottle on the draining-board and lifting its neck. The business of filling it required care, the hot water had a disconcerting way of spurting out which always made her jump and drop everything. This time, however, caution paid off and she took the stopper, giving it the four preliminary turns anti-clockwise necessary to prevent the string which attached it to the neck of the bottle from becoming twisted, and screwed it in firmly. Finally, she slipped the bottle into one of the old woollen covers made by Val when she had been learning to knit, pulled the drawstring tight, and went quickly up the stairs.

Going into Josephine's room was like stepping out from shelter on to a snow-covered hillside - the spare white tidiness of it still took her breath away. An archangel's consulting-room was how she had once described it when they had been discussing plans for re-decoration and she had wanted to change the colour of the walls for something warmer: "or at least new *curtains*", old rose perhaps - like the beautiful curtains Albina had chosen for the main bedroom in her new home when she was getting married - or chrysanthemum red, anything but this implacable slate blue which hung so austerely down to the grey carpet. Iris folded the blue-grey bedspread and put it on the chair by the window then, with hospital precision, she turned back the bedclothes (no sprawl of duvet for Josephine) and slipped the hot-water bottle between the sheets to where she judged her back would be. She glanced round the room again and, with a regretful ts-ts of her tongue, went downstairs to the sitting-room.

Josephine had not moved. The only indication that anything might have happened during Iris's absence was that her face was a moist crimson streaked with wisps of damp hair, and she was gasping for breath.

"I can't move, Iris. I'm stuck."

"You can't be." Tall and broad she might be but she certainly was not fat, her body didn't even fill the chair.

"I am. I can't budge."

"Hold on to me." Josephine gripped her hands, and Iris winced: there was no weakness there. She braced herself against the chair leg and tried to pull her to her feet, but Josephine's superior height meant superior weight as well and, tug as she might, Iris could not shift her. Josephine had sat in her chair for what seemed like a week and now she might just as well have been welded there.

"I'll have to phone the doctor."

"The doctor? How can he help? I don't need a doctor."

"Well, I'll have to get someone. Let me pop next

door for Margery."

"Certainly not. You're being feeble, Iris. Come here. Now, put your arms round my waist."

Iris stood in front of her and bent forward obediently, arms outstretched. Her fingertips touched behind Josephine's back and, with short bursts of stretching, she was able to clasp them in some sort of embrace. Then, with Josephine's hands locked behind her neck, she gave a mighty heave. Nothing happened. To an observer it would have looked as if neither of them had made any effort at all. Josephine was right. She did not budge. Again Iris heaved and again nothing happened. They tried counting to synchronise their efforts: "One, two, three, *heave!*" but to no avail.

"It's no good, Jo. I'll have to get help. I can't move you by myself."

"Iris!" Josephine glared at her.

"You can't just sit there. You ought to be in bed, you said so yourself."

"Give me the phone."

"Who are you going to ring?"

"Give me the phone. I shall get Val to come home."

"You can't do that - she's in the middle of her exams! You can't disturb her like that."

"Yes, I can. Give me the phone!"

It couldn't do any harm, Iris reasoned, glancing at the clock, Val would be safely in the examination hall by now. She lifted the telephone from its corner by the window-seat and put it on the table next to Josephine's chair.

"You'll have to dial for me." Iris dialled and handed her the receiver. Evidently someone answered.

"Val? Val, yes, it's me. Listen, you'll have to come at once."

"*Jo!*" Iris was appalled.

"Well, never mind that, you'll have to come. Mother's useless. I'm stuck here in this damned chair and she's not man enough to get me out. You'll have to come and help. What? No, I'm not ill. I'm dying. Certainly not. You know what I think of doctors. Yes, I know I'm a doctor, dear... yes, and you're a doctor... and Edwin too. Well, you and Mother ought to be able to manage it between you, but she's useless. You've got to come immediately."

"Jo!" Iris snatched the receiver from her and, seizing the telephone, marched across the room to the window-seat.

"Val dear, it's me. I'm sorry about this." She could hear the anxiety in Val's voice.

"What's happening? What on earth's going on?"

"It's all right, darling. Tell me, why aren't you in your exams?"

"I don't have any today, Mum. It's tomorrow."

"Oh dear, what day is it? I seem to have lost track of time a bit. I thought you had more than one?"

"Only one written exam. Clinicals and Orals aren't till next month. Mum, forget the exams... you can tell me: is Jo really dying?"

"I don't know, dear. She says she is, and you know what she's like once she gets an idea in her head. But I don't think she's going just yet. She's a bit stiff. That's all."

"A bit stiff!" Josephine snorted.

"And I'm having something of a problem getting her out of her chair, but it'll be all right. If I need help, I'll get Margery."

"Over my dead body!"

"Are you sure she's all right? You don't want me to come home? I could get home tonight."

"Now listen, darling... I can manage."

"Huh!"

"You mustn't worry... she's all right. Just you finish your exams. I'll telephone you this evening."

"Well... if you're sure..."

"Yes, I'm sure. Don't worry, darling. Really. Good luck..." she had been going to say "with the exam" but recollected herself. "Good luck. Jo sends love." Josephine snorted again. "I'll ring you tonight about eight o'clock. 'Bye." Iris waited for Val to replace the receiver before hanging up. She turned.

"Jo, how could you upset her like that? And in the middle of her exams?"

"Well, I'm dying."

"No, you're not dying. Not yet, anyway. Now be quiet and let me think."

It seemed unlikely that she would be able to move Josephine by herself, and the idea of setting up a sort of rocking motion between them and swinging her up and out of her chair fell apart when, in her mind's eye, she saw them both topple over and roll about on the floor like a couple of brawling urchins. The notion of an elderly urchin distracted her momentarily. Perhaps she could tip her out of the chair on to her knees, then get her to her feet somehow or, if that didn't work, help her to crawl across the room and through the hall and up the... Iris turned her head away and blinked rapidly. No... that would not do.

"Suppose I tried pushing you in the chair. It

moves all right when I'm hoovering." But under Josephine's weight the domes of silence were embedded too deeply in the carpet, and the chair remained emphatically where it was. Josephine struggled to get up.

"Jo, for goodness' sake stop it. Just sit still for a minute."

"I am bloody well sitting still. I can't seem to do anything else. Iris, do something, please... I don't want to stay here for ever."

"That's not what you said the other day."

"That was the other day. Now I want to go to bed. I want to go to bed... *now*!"

"All right. All right. I have an idea. You'll have to wait while I go and have a look..."

"What for, for God's sake? You're not sneaking off for Margery, are you?"

"No. Now just wait. I won't be a minute."

"Well, buck up, love."

It was little more than a whisper now, in fact there was something almost wistful about it. Once, it had been a clarion summons, reveillé, a breezy command from a Viking woman to banish the blues and the past along with them: "Buck up, love." Incisively, the voice had sliced through the clamour of wind and sea and engines and what was going on in her own head and heart. "I said my good-byes yesterday." And it had been plain that for this tall woman, with her dark hair stirring in the wind as the liner got under way, the past had already been put firmly in its place. Iris had turned her tear-streaked face to look up at her and had hated her.

It was strange how that injunction, more of a figure of speech really than a command (although

Josephine could be pretty commanding at times) ruffled the still surface of memory, strange what power it had, even now, to conjure up the wretchedness of those early days on board ship. She wondered what had become of the ship, that vast ocean-going hold-all of a vessel, stuffed with all those £10 optimists bound for Australia. Iris had not been one of them: oh, she had paid her £10 all right, but she had not been travelling particularly hopefully, and her passage to the land of opportunity had cost her considerably more than that.

She realised that she had been rummaging about in the broom cupboard under the stairs for far longer than was necessary since what she was looking for was manifestly not there. That's what happened when you set out on voyages of the mind, she told herself sharply, and she straightened the broom-handles and mops, and tucked an ancient carpet-sweeper back into its resting-place behind the hoover before closing the door.

"Shan't be long," she called out, and hurried through the kitchen, lifting the keys from the hook by the back door as she stepped out into the garden. She took no account of the day, her sights being set on the garden shed where, once inside, she searched through a half wigwam of planks and discarded shelving and other pieces of wood stacked against the rear wall, while her mind, ignoring her recent strictures on time-wasting, focussed again on that distant odyssey, bringing every detail of it so vividly to her attention that even the seat of Val's old swing, seamed and shiny with use, and itself a potent reminder of a different past, could not draw her back from this latest voyage down the long sea-lanes of memory.

She had been lying in her bed in the ship's hospital, weeping into a towel - her pillow was sodden. Self-pity on this fourth - or was it fifth? - day had finally got the better of her and, linking arms with indecision and a newly realised sense of loss, had reduced her to the helpless tears of childhood.

"May I come in?"

She had turned over, peering through a tangle of hair and tears, and had mumbled an incoherent "yes" before she recognised the tall figure of her enemy.

"Oh Lord." She remembered scrambling about in the bed in a muddled effort to sit up and unwind her nightdress and generally tidy herself and dry her eyes all at the same time. "We always seem to meet when I'm blubbing." Not a word she would normally have chosen but it sounded appropriate then.

'Don't rush. Don't rush. Sorry to startle you." There was none of the abrasiveness she remembered; in fact, the voice was gentle. "Dr. Reid said you might be in need of a spot of company. I'm Josephine Jackson... Jo..." the laugh was unabrasive too and attractively throaty, "Dr. Jo Jackson." It was several days before Iris realised that she had not been using the title figuratively. "He told me about the baby. I'm sorry. You must be feeling rotten."

Iris managed a wintry smile: "I don't know why. It's just today... quite suddenly... I can't seem to stop. Post baby blues, Sister says. Ironical, isn't it? No baby, but post..." The attempt at humour failed, and she was crying again.

"Here... have a hanky." Josephine put an arm round her shoulders and blew her nose for her like a child. "It's quite normal, you know, and in your case perfectly understandable. Listen... do you play Scrabble? I've got a Scrabble board in my cabin. It might help take your mind off things."

So they played Scrabble and talked, or Iris had talked and Josephine had listened, asking a question here and there, but mostly listening while Iris talked. Feverish talk, unwise, compulsive, as though she were starving and to speak was eating... as though her life depended on it. And perhaps it did. Dr. Reid had diagnosed her condition accurately when he mentioned to Josephine that he had a patient who might be in need of a friend. She told her about Nick. "He didn't know I was pregnant. I'm sure he'd have done the..." she made quote signs with her fingers "...honourable thing, if he had." She had no doubt of it. "But it would have been a compromise and... and I couldn't risk it." She looked apologetically at Josephine who had the clear-eyed expression of someone for whom compromises, or the need for them, or indeed any sort of problem at all, quite simply did not arise. "I suppose I've always been a bit unlucky in love... I'm not all that lucky at cards either..." she smiled as she remembered saying it, "and Nick was so kind..." she used to think he was the first truly kind man she had met "...a sort of uncomplicated goodness." It had been most attractive. And of course it had been that very kindness which had prevented him from leaving his wife and children for her. "He loved me, and he loved them too. It *is* possible, you know." She laughed a small, self-deprecating laugh.

Josephine nodded.

It had all started so innocently - a cup of coffee, a drink after work, a concert... nothing to it... and that was how it had remained for a long time, and all that time love had been working like some underground river, eroding the substructures until there she was, fragile as a honeycomb.

Iris blushed now - as she had done many times at the memory of that day - and pounced on a piece of wood of exactly the size and shape she was looking for. The blush nudged her back to the present, and she seized the plank and hastened back to the house, almost forgetting to lock the shed door in her hurry. "Oh dear, I hope I haven't been away for ages. Poor Jo."

However, Josephine had dozed off. Iris stopped in front of her, undecided for a moment, and in that moment had one of those rare instances of revelation, seeing her as if for the first time, uncluttered by images from the past. The face was handsome rather than beautiful, there was not much about it that was soft or compliant, and although there were plenty of lines wrought by humour there were also lines indicative of impatience and self-will. It was an imperious face even in repose. In repose, though, Josephine looked younger, not quite the Viking woman of nearly forty years ago, of course, but still with something of her vitality. I don't know why I called her a Viking when she was so dark. It must have been her height and that marvellous, fearless way she had - has - of confronting the world... and her face. Iris shook her gently.

"My God, you're not going to hit me with that thing, are you?"

"Don't be silly. I'm going to try and lever you out."

"Huh. The Almighty's right-hand dentist levering

out a rotten tooth, I suppose. Oh well, lever away."

It puzzled Iris how Josephine, who had always been so active, so effortlessly good at everything, could have come to this pass in such a short time. Until a few days ago she had still played a round of golf every week, to a respectable handicap, as well as doing most of the gardening, certainly most of the heavy work. And even though she no longer drove up to London, she was to be seen striding the two and a half miles to the station to catch the train for a once-a-month trip to stay with Val or meet old friends and visit old haunts; although nowadays, she had admitted ruefully, the haunts were beginning to outnumber the friends - Iris went too, from time to time, but she didn't really care for London, and preferred to see Val when she came home - and in all these activities there had never been the least sign of any diminution in vigour. She didn't seem to get unduly tired or doze off in her wing chair of an evening as Iris sometimes did. It could only be, Iris surmised, that the abrupt cessation of all action, even for so relatively short a time - less than a week after all - had resulted in a complete mechanical breakdown, with none of the moving parts - or none so far as she could tell - moving with any facility any more. Certainly, from the waist downwards everything, spine, hips, knees, ankles - toe-joints too - had seized up to such an extent that by the time Iris had finally succeeded in wedging the short plank into a workable position a considerable amount of it had passed. Nor had she been much helped by Josephine's efforts to help herself by pushing up on the arms of her chair. However, now at last she was able to get some purchase on the thing. She braced herself, took a deep breath, and lunged on her end of the plank. And, quite suddenly, Josephine was vertical. She wobbled dangerously, and Iris held her breath, not daring to relinquish her hold on the plank; and then, miraculously it seemed, she righted herself. Iris breathed again.

"I don't know about you, but I could use a cup of tea," Josephine announced, red-faced and cheerful, from her new position.

"Couldn't you have said that before I got you on your feet?" Iris didn't even try to keep the crossness out of her voice. "Don't you *dare* sit down again!" Josephine had so far forgotten herself as to be about to flop triumphantly back into her seat. Iris thumped the plank down across the arms of the chair. She would have nailed it there if she could, and Josephine with it.

"I wasn't thirsty then."

"Well, just don't dare sit down again. Here, I'll turn the chair round so you can prop yourself up against the back. And try to loosen up a bit. Try moving your legs or bending your knees or something. I wish you'd let me fetch Margery."

"Certainly not."

"We don't want to spend all day getting you upstairs."

"We don't *want* to do *anything*."

While she was making the tea, Iris crammed a biscuit into her mouth. At least Josephine was separated from that wretched chair. "Do you want something to eat?" she called, spraying biscuit crumbs over the draining-board. There was no answer. "If you're not going to die till you get upstairs you'll need a bit of sustenance." She swept the crumbs into the sink. "Would you like a biscuit?"

"Do me some toast and Bovril."

"That's invalid food. Are you sure?"

"I *am* an invalid."

Iris marched back into the sitting-room with two mugs of tea. "I don't know what's got into you, Jo. First, all this business about dying, and now about being an invalid. You're as strong as an ox... stronger than I am, probably."

"I don't see why. I'm years older than you."

"That has nothing to do with it, as well you know. And what's happened to commonsense all of a sudden? Or is that the *real* casualty here?"

She put the mugs down on the plank, and returned to the kitchen for the toast. This obsession with dying was so unlike Josephine: living had been the thing. She had never had much truck with what she called "the old adversary" - "professional failure", had been her verdict on more than one occasion, "except in the case of the aged" (which was definitely not how she saw herself) and her strictures on the subject had become something of a by-word. Once, she had exclaimed with more ferocity than logic: "It's an affront... against nature... against life... against *God*!" And Iris had tried to reason with her: "There's nothing you could have done about Albina. You know that. You did all you possibly could... more." And Josephine had become silent. Now, however, it was as if she wanted to confront her adversary... as if, for these past days and nights, from the fastness of her wing chair, she had challenged him to do his worst, and she had won. Was that it? Had Josephine triumphed over death? Iris could quite believe it.

"Now," she took away the plate and mugs, "do you think, if you lean on me, you could walk?"

The trouble was that Josephine was weak as well as stiff, and the effort required to raise her feet in their sheepskin house boots (Iris had unthinkingly once referred to them as bootees, and still trembled at the recollection) was such that progress was reduced to a leaden shuffle. Josephine was beginning to lose patience.

"Can't you move any faster, Iris?"

"I'm sorry. It's really a question of keeping time with you. You're a mite unsteady, you know." Not only that, but *tall* and unsteady. "I don't want you to fall. Suppose I move your feet for you, one at a time to make a bigger step... d'you think that would work?"

"You can try."

Iris knelt down and edged one foot forward a few inches. The carpet was not very even. "How does that feel?"

"Most peculiar." Josephine glared down at her. "I know how Gulliver must've felt."

"I wish we had a walking frame. Perhaps Margery..."

"Oh no you don't! I'm not having one of those things, they're for geriatrics! I'll get up the stairs under my own steam, or not at all."

After several more attempts they fell into a kind of rhythm: Iris would kneel down and inch Josephine's foot forward, working it from side to side to advance it gently until it was a reasonable step in front of the other - at all costs she wanted to avoid any sudden lurches - then she would stand up to steady the ominous swaying motion while Josephine transferred her weight to the other foot, then steady her again before kneeling down to repeat the sequence. It was slow and laborious, but it worked.

"Hell! I don't have to learn to *walk*, for God's sake!"

"I thought of the Himalaya when I was in the shed."

"What? Whatever made you think of them? You're not on about the epic journey again, are you?"

"Not the mountains, silly... the S.S. Himalaya."

"Stop babbling, Iris, I'm concentrating." They advanced two more steps. "Boiled beet and carrot."

"What's that?"

"That's what you looked like that day, you poor old thing... boiled beetroot and carrot. It's a good job Val made you do something about your hair... you'd be milk-white all over, otherwise... very unappetising."

"Don't be rude."

The rudeness proved to be an excellent propellant, however, and for the next few steps they were in danger of gathering speed, although Iris did have to admit that it was all relative.

"You seem to remember everything." Josephine wiped her forehead with the back of her hand. "God, I'm hot. I thought I remembered everything." Another step. "I'll tell you what I do remember, though." Josephine stopped.

"Don't stop now, Jo, please."

"Something I haven't thought of in years. I remember sitting on a milking-stool by the kitchen door in my grandmother's house reading 'Black Beauty' and I was crying... Ginger had died... and Mother left what she was doing and came and read to me. I sat on the sofa beside her and she read on a bit about a little pony and cart. She stopped getting the lunch ready and came and read to me. Father wasn't there, he must've been out on a call. I don't know where the boys were, they'd never have let me forget it if they'd been around - blubbing over a book!" She started to move again. "I don't ever remember crying like that... I don't think I ever have since."

Iris was concentrating and didn't really know what that had to do with anything, except that if it kept Josephine going she supposed that relevance or irrelevance didn't matter. Kneel down, inch forward, stand up, steady, steady again, kneel down. It was like trying to move a tower of building blocks without toppling them. "'Buck up, love', you said."

"Sh'sh."

Perhaps because it had been so uncharacteristic of her, Iris still remembered that sudden burst of hatred. For a moment it had obliterated despair. So vivid had been the image of Nick receding on the quayside that she had forgotten he was not actually there, or that she had refused to let him come to see her off and had, like the Viking woman beside her, said her good-byes the day before, or the only good-bye which had mattered. Her mother and sister were there to be sure, waving farewell to the strains of 'A Life on the Ocean Wave', but it was Nick whom she had seen dwindling and growing fainter in the fading light of that winter afternoon and, blinded suddenly by hatred and other more complicated emotions, she had pushed her way back through the crowd at the rail before he should disappear altogether.

Common interests, a love of music and books, had first drawn them together: the occasional concert in the Wigmore or Albert or Festival Halls, the occasional harmless lunch or brief browse in a bookshop had led gradually to encounters less innocent, albeit guiltless enough in their content, and more frequent. And these, in their turn, had led to an affair which had become the delight and, much later, the despair of her life. So complete had been her faith in her power to keep emotion under control, in her ability to accept things as they were without ever wishing to change them that, like many a sensible young woman in love with a married man, by the time she realised just how wrong she was it was too late. And that was even before she had discovered that she was pregnant. After that, she wanted to change everything.

It had been some time before she had been able to reach any decision about what she should do. In the end she had discarded all the obvious options open to her and had chosen instead to salvage what she could, at the expense of love: she would put as much distance as possible - half the world seemed reasonable - between her and Nick. In Australia, she could pretend to a recent widowhood and have her baby in comparative anonymity. She might even settle there.

Once decided upon, her plans went forward with the same relentless efficiency as that with which the S.S. Himalaya forged a passage through the oceans, her destiny out of her hands. The final weeks in England, with their farewells and their few, all too brief, meetings with Nick had come and gone in a permanent cold ache of cold weather, cold hands and feet, cold stomach and colder tears.

And then, two weeks out in a voyage

unremarkable save for that same unremitting chill - even the sight of the Suez Canal had failed to warm her and surprised only by its very unremarkableness - her sleep had been disturbed by a spasm of pain. Wide awake, she had waited, but nothing happened. After a while she drowsed and would have fallen asleep again when another spasm jolted her into wakefulness, then another, and another, each becoming slowly more insistent throughout the remainder of the night and the hours that followed, until a sudden flux and a warm slithery movement between her legs told her that what she had been denying to herself all day was a fact.

Had it not been for the timely arrival of Dr. Josephine Jackson at her bedside a few days later, heaven knew what she might or might not have done. All her plans, and such hopes as she had permitted herself had been centred on her baby and, without it, she could envisage no future. She had more than half thought of slipping over the side of the huge ship into the dark, warm, beautiful Indian Ocean. Dr. Jackson had changed all that but she could not change Iris who, with each day that passed, oscillated between the growing realisation that there was nothing now to stop her returning to England and Nick - if he would have her - and the diminishing notion of making a life for herself in Australia. She had confided in Josephine.

"What a waste!" Josephine had leapt to her feet, making Iris jump. "A wicked, shameful waste! Of you, of opportunity, of *life*!" She smacked her hand, palm down, on the table. "Don't you know what you'd be going back to? What you've just had the guts to leave. What's so bloody marvellous about it?"

She threw up both hands. "I knew you were a bit wet, but I never had you marked down for an idiot!"

And all the hatred had come flooding back and, with it, an anger so intense that it roared in her head making her dizzy. She could feel it still. What business was it of hers? That arrogant, interfering - there was no other word for it - bitch! What did she know about anything? She wanted to hit her, to pommel her senseless. Just because she was a doctor!

Josephine had stayed away.

Iris was discharged from the hospital and began, for the first time on the voyage, to take a tentative part in shipboard life: a little judicious sunbathing - with her fair skin and red hair she had to be sensible - a little swimming, even some dancing. Sometimes she saw Josephine in the distance, but Josephine appeared not to see her. Always her tall figure was the focus of an animated group of people, men mostly. Once, Iris had heard laughter and had looked round to see her with her head tilted back in a laugh of such pure delight that what remained of anger and hatred had fizzled out, leaving her feeling light with happiness. Josephine caught her eye, and by the time the ship had reached Fremantle, plans were well under way for a life in Melbourne which, to her surprise, she had begun to look forward to.

"What on earth made you think of that?"

Iris started. "What?"

"The Himalaya."

"You don't remember standing beside me when we left Tilbury?"

"Nope."

"You said…"

Josephine interrupted: "I know what you said I

said." She chuckled. "I'm damn glad I didn't have anyone waving good-bye to *me*. I've never seen such a ghastly sight!"

"What about Piraeus, then? Do you remember Piraeus? That really was awful." Iris was making conversation. There was no doubt about it, the feet moved more readily when Josephine was distracted from trying quite so hard. "I can see them now. All those old women in black - at least they looked old - all crying, and everyone clinging to each other in the sunshine. The sunshine made it worse somehow. And the luggage... those battered suitcases, do you remember? And all those gaily painted boxes tied round with cord. It was heartbreaking."

"I remember Aussie Customs ripping open the hems of their clothes."

"Poor things, you couldn't really call it smuggling... just a handful of seeds and stuff from home."

"They must have known it was illegal."

"I know, poor souls. And after they came on board they just disappeared, do you remember? Five hundred people just vanished. Except for the Greek evening, and a woman I saw breast-feeding her baby, we never saw them after Piraeus until Melbourne, having their precious things torn apart. It really was vast, the Himalaya, wasn't it? It just swallowed them up. I used to go to the reading room, and often I was the only person there."

"I enjoyed that trip."

"Yes... it's funny... looking back on it now, so did I. At the time I couldn't remember when I'd been more miserable, seeing all those people on the quayside getting smaller and smaller and not knowing when you'd see them again, and the wind, and that dreadful, jolly music booming out over the tannoys. We were all supposed to be going to a brave new world." She was silent, snaring stray strands of memory. "Do you remember, I asked you what you were running away from?"

"Did you?"

"And you…" Iris glanced up at Josephine's face, remembering the expression on it, "'Not everyone on this ship is running away, Iris'," and the frosty way she had of saying her name. "That's what you said."

"I'm trying to concentrate, Iris. Do shut up."

Iris had wondered why someone like Josephine should have chosen, at the age of nearly forty, to pull up her roots and go to the other end of the earth. It wouldn't be difficult to guess to some extent at the curiosity and the seeming lack of fear and the appetite for life which must have taken her from the eminently safe city of Bath to places more outlandish than anything she herself could begin to imagine or wish to experience. On the other hand, there seemed to be no rational explanation for leaving home and work when these provided the perfect springboard for such adventures. Why would she want to change the pattern completely all of a sudden? She had been offered an interesting post in Melbourne, she said, and Iris had nodded her head, not entirely convinced.

Josephine had been in general practice in Bath with her father and his younger partner. Her mother was dead. Her home was a comfortable, self-contained apartment on the top two floors of her father's house in the Circus, and when he died, less than a year after her arrival in Australia, Iris had fully expected her to return to England to take up the reins where she had left them. As it was, she flew home for the funeral, stayed for a week, and then flew back again to Melbourne without a word (nor did she encourage sympathy or any discussion of the subject) and their life there had continued much as before.

"Damn!"

They had come to a halt. For a while each step had been requiring a greater effort from them both for less result, and now Josephine's feet refused to move, having become stuck in what Iris could only assume was a more luxuriant patch of pile in the otherwise elderly carpet. "You'd have thought at least we might have worn a path to the door," she grumbled, half to herself and half out loud. She had noticed that Josephine was getting short of breath, and that, coupled with the swaying when Iris wasn't up at her side to steady her, was beginning to alarm her. She had suggested fetching a walking-stick, but Josephine was adamant: "No. No. *No*! How many more times do I have to say it?" If she could just think of something to keep her going until they reached the doorway.

"When I'm hoovering, I always think this patch here looks like Australia." She gestured towards a spot a step or two ahead of them. "It'll be quite bald soon."

"Rubbish. It'll see us both out."

"Don't you think it looks a bit like Australia?"

"All bare patches look like Australia. Australia looks like a bare patch of carpet."

"Do you ever regret leaving?"

"Iris." It sounded like a warning, but Iris was beginning to feel lightheaded with all the kneeling down and standing up. Besides, it was now well past lunch-time and, apart from her biscuit in the kitchen earlier, she had had nothing to eat since breakfast, and breakfast had been a bowl of cereal hours ago.

"Non, rien de rien. Non, je ne regrette rien," she carolled. Could anyone have nothing to regret? Was it humanly possible? She had regrets: to this day there were things she regretted although, now that she came to think of it, the loss of her baby was no longer one of them. Nature had done its job properly and had expelled a defective foetus, Dr. Reid had been very specific about that. But Mervyn... ah, yes, Mervyn... dear Mervyn: in that hour between the first and second sleeps, sometimes she regretted him; but then, if she had dug in her toes, everything might have been - undoubtedly would have been - different. And there were things which Josephine ought to have regretted of course, but she didn't. Iris knew that. Just as she knew that the same clear-eyed way of looking at the world coloured everything for Josephine. Regret was self-indulgent and unproductive, she would have said, it reeked of self-examination, and as such was to be eschewed - not necessarily suppressed or unhealthily repressed, but exploded, ionised, magicked to nothingness. And Josephine had the trick of it if anybody did.

They had reached the doorway.

"At last! Only another couple of steps and you can sit on the stairs. Do you want the loo before we get there?" It was a mystery how Josephine had managed for all that time, but apparently she had, so perhaps it was best not to enquire.

"Might as well." -

Two steps was, as everything else seemed to be today, an under-estimation; however, another quarter of an hour saw Josephine, whose limbs, notwithstanding setbacks, had loosened up slightly during the journey from her chair, sink down with such a heavy sigh of relief on to the lavatory in the cloakroom that Iris wondered whether this might not indeed be the final resting-place she professed to be so ready for. She waited.

"It's no use, Iris, I can't do anything."

"Stay there a bit longer. Give it a chance."

"It won't be any use." Josephine made as if to get up.

"Stay there. I must have a biscuit or something. I'm starving. Shall I make us some more tea?"

"I refuse to eat in the lavatory. Get yourself a biscuit, if you must. Some of us can go a whole week without food." Iris ignored the exaggeration. "I shall have something when I reach the stairs."

"Have you thought about how you're going to get up them?"

"The usual way?"

"Well, unless your knees get a lot more flexible, the usual way is out. I think you're going to have to sit down and sort of bump yourself up."

"How do you mean, bump myself up?"

"Well, like bumping down, but in reverse. Use your arms to lift yourself one stair at a time, and bring your feet up after you."

"Right." Josephine sat in silence. "Right. If that's how it's got to be done, that's how it's got to be done." She waved a hand grandly.

Iris heard a trickle in the lavatory pan and, before Josephine could stop her, escaped to the kitchen. She hoped she wasn't being over-optimistic about the next leg of their journey. She filled the kettle and switched it on before taking a digestive biscuit from the tin and slipping two more into her apron pocket where they rustled against the morning's post.

"Gracious, I completely forgot." She bustled back to the hall. "I had a letter from Mervyn today... I haven't even opened it yet. Do you want me to read it to you?"

"Not now. Save it for later."

Despite the improvement Iris had noticed earlier, Josephine was stuck again. In an attempt to raise herself from her magisterial position she had seized the washbasin and was pulling on it.

"Jo, stop it, for goodness' sake. You'll have it off the wall." Iris squeezed round behind her and, without ceremony, half lifted and half pushed her to her feet, grabbing her trousers before they hit the floor and making them secure. Then, once more, they set off. By the time they reached the foot of the stairs, they were both out of breath.

"A bit like the foothills of the Himalayas," panted Josephine, nodding over her shoulder towards the staircase with rather more cheerfulness than Iris felt was justified, as she prepared to subside on to the bottom step.

"Try to aim a bit higher up," Iris gasped. "Hold on to me and I'll let you down slowly. There. Now you won't have so far to climb later."

"Whew!" Josephine was sweating.

"Now... tea, I think. Do you want biscuits, or shall I make some toast and honey? I think you ought to have something sweet."

"*I'm* the doctor around here! I'll have toast and honey... only a scraping of butter."

"Are you feeling all right?"

"Absolutely bloody marvellous! What do you think?"

Chapter 2

"The trouble with M-E-N is that they're the opposite sex, or they believe they are." Josephine placed an O, then two P's, followed by another O and an S above the E of Iris's modest three-letter word.

"Ye-es?" Facing her was a row of seven impossible letters, all consonants.

"I have four brothers and I know they're not, but people make assumptions."

"N-O-T. I'm sorry, I haven't any vowels. How so, not?"

"Opposite. Opposed, opposition, unlike, as night is to day, friend and foe, the enemy. We've all been brain-washed, brought up to think that way."

"Surely not?" Iris sighed at the sight of two more consonants. "Of course, we *are* the weaker sex."

Josephine set down her letters with particular emphasis. "Of course nothing of the sort! There's no 'of course' about it. They are strong, we are stronger. Think of it. In every way except size and mere brute strength *we* are stronger. Emotionally. Physiologically. We live longer."

"But how about intellectually?"

"Equals. That's how the Almighty intended it. And not equal and opposite either. Equal and different. Although, if you think about it, even there the similarities far outweigh the differences."

Iris couldn't help admiring such certitude, born, she was sure, of those early years spent in the company of four brothers; and yet, often as she thought about it, she had never been able properly to envisage those early years. The boys laughed down at her from the branches of an apple tree, or waved from sailing dinghies, or shouted and did hand-stands in meadows of ox-eye daisies, but Josephine was not in the photo with them. Josephine had sprung into the world fully armed, in one giant leap from Jupiter's head.

Iris's own early life had produced no certainties. Rather, it seemed in retrospect to have been woven from the fine threads of other people's disappointment, mostly their disappointment in *her*: in her failure to have been born a boy or, failing that, a tomboy; in her failure to be as pretty or as amenable or as clever as her sister Rose, or as amenable and clever and pretty as her mother would have liked her to be (nor did her mother care much for red hair); in her failure to marry and, having failed there, to reach that peak in her career which would have made all the other failures tolerable. She was, her mother never tired of reminding her, her father's daughter, giving Iris to understand that he had failed that lady's expectation of him from the day that they were married until he died, too soon to make amends. Small failures, in part inherited, in part nurtured, none of them large enough to stand by themselves, but all contributing to a pervasive diffidence which she had neither understood nor managed completely to overcome. She would, occasionally, gaze at her image in the mirror, and her image would smile at her reassuringly, and she knew that it lied.

To Josephine, however, everything seemed to come easily and, as if by magic, everything had started to come more easily to Iris as well. In her new life in Melbourne, undertakings which would normally have filled her with dismay, or at the very least with apprehension, were discharged almost effortlessly, so that even the most mundane chores acquired a pleasurable gloss. Together with Josephine she had found a flat for them both on their first day ashore and, as if that wasn't wonder enough, before the week was out she had secured a post teaching English at a day school for girls while Josephine, who already had a job waiting for her, had bought a car. Once installed in their new home, with their new careers and new friendship embarked upon, they settled to the delightful business of exploring a new city and a new country. Before the year had ended, Josephine had taught her to drive, and not only had she surprised herself (although not Josephine) by passing the driving test at her first attempt but, elated by this achievement, she too had bought a car.

Later, when events had given her cause to look back, Iris had seen that it must have been from about this time that their life together had begun subtly to change. Of course, it was only to be expected with two such different temperaments, she had told herself. "Get a car. Learn to drive," Nick used to advise her when he was worrying, as he frequently did, about her solitary life, "you'll be able to get out more." Iris hadn't minded the solitariness, and she could have gone out more had she so wished. In the dream-like days on her own when she hadn't wanted to change anything, often she could not tell whether hours or minutes had passed, and it didn't matter. The solitariness only served to enhance those times which they were able to spend with each other. It was Nick who worried about it.

Having two cars had meant that Josephine began

to spend more of her spare time away from home, while Iris's concerns became increasingly domestic. Josephine made expeditions - days, weekends, sometimes a week or more of her leave, were spent driving farther and still farther into the heart of that alien land. Iris went to concerts or visited friends, usually, like her, from England. The games of Scrabble, once so much a feature of their evenings together, became fewer and fewer until, after Josephine's return from her father's funeral, they had ceased altogether and the board was finally packed away. In time this new version of their life took on a pattern and harmony of its own. Josephine appeared to be contented with it and Iris, who certainly was not *un*happy, no more expected it to change than she would have expected Brighton suddenly to be Bournemouth in a stick of seaside rock.

Then, one morning at breakfast, Josephine had announced: "I'm thinking of changing my job," and Iris knew that if that was what she was thinking it was as good as decided.

"Anything in particular?" she had enquired, trying to sound casual.

"The Flying Doctor Service."

"The Flying Doctor Service?" If she had said the Foreign Legion Iris could not have been more astonished. "The Flying Doctor Service? Won't that mean leaving Melbourne?"

"I'll be based at Broken Hill. Don't worry though, you don't have to come. You're pretty well settled here, aren't you?"

Iris scrambled around in her head trying to make contact with one coherent thought. "Will you want to keep the flat on?"

"Oh, I think so. I'll be popping down for weekends and holidays, that sort of thing. I need a change."

And away she had gone.

Thoughtfully Iris scraped some butter on the toast as instructed. She was more lavish with the honey though, it was just too bad if it all dribbled off onto the plate.

She had missed her. Josephine's was a presence you couldn't fail to miss even though quite often she wasn't physically there anyway. It was like having the electricity cut off, a dimension had been removed from life and it had taken her time to adjust, time to acknowledge that it hurt. Josephine had seemed not to want her to go with her - the thought that it would have been extremely inconvenient if she *had* wanted her to, had afforded her no comfort whatsoever. She wondered if it was something she had done, or perhaps failed to do. It had certainly never occurred to her with any conviction that it might simply be Josephine. More than one night was passed in wakefulness, going over the three years they had spent together, trying to recall conversations they had had, in an attempt to turn up clues, to understand what it was that had happened. She could guess at a certain restlessness from the pattern of Josephine's life before they had met, from stories of the things she had done, things which Iris, even with examples of intrepid Victorian lady travellers like Mary Kingsley in mind, found it hard to imagine a woman doing. Josephine had once spent a whole month skiing across Lapland, and on another expedition had taken a canoe up the Amazon - not completely alone, of course, but even so..! There were stories of journeys without so much as a one-star hotel or a bathroom in any of them, journeys which Josephine, if she was to be believed (and Iris saw no reason not to) had actually relished. It was a pattern which had been interrupted so often that those very interruptions had come to be part of it until the day when she had disrupted it completely and had departed for Australia. But for some reason (the very baselessness of which was perfectly clear now) she hadn't believed that Josephine would do it again. And because they had come to lead lives which were broadly independent of each other, she hadn't realised just how closely those lives were knit together, or how closely hers had been knit with Josephine's, how dependent on her she had become. And then, seemingly without a thought for anything or anyone, Josephine had abandoned her and, yes, it hurt. And it took time to plug the hole left by that departure, time to piece together a different life for herself.

Chapter 3

"I thought Mervyn was married, you know."

Josephine sniffed contemptuously. They had finished their snack and she was wiping honey off the plate with her finger and licking it.

"It never occurred to me that he might live with his mother. Did you meet his mother?"

"Nope." Josephine was still licking her fingers. "What was she like? No, don't tell me, let me guess. The original all-purpose Aussie woman, an elderly sheila, plain and pioneering."

Iris shook her head. "Not really. She was very capable, of course. You'd have liked her. There was no nonsense about her."

"Not one of the pillars of Toorak society who went bananas when Jean Shrimpton let the side down at the Melbourne Cup? The hat and gloves-to-go-shopping brigade?"

"No. Much more easy-going than that." Iris frowned. "We were back here by then."

"What?"

"When Jean Shrimpton wore her mini skirt to the races, we were back here."

"Were we?"

"Yes. Mervyn wrote and told us about it. Don't you remember? No, she was nice... nice looking too. Very direct. You didn't have to wonder what she was thinking, it came straight out of her mouth... she fairly took your breath away with some of the things she said. I think Mervyn was a bit of a puzzle to her." She thought of something else: "He sent us that cutting, don't you remember? Of Jean Shrimpton at the Melbourne Cup?"

Josephine chuckled. "Oh yes. All those hot, cross women!"

"She didn't have a clue about music, but she was very proud of him. She didn't have a clue about him either, really. He's a solitary sort of man, and she liked company... the Bowls Club, that sort of thing. She did a lot of voluntary work... the R.S.L. mainly. She liked me, I think. It always surprised me rather. She used to say Mervyn and I ought to get married." Josephine grunted. "Yes, it was quite embarrassing. But I suppose marriage was something she understood, even though she'd been widowed for years. Her daughter was married, you know... Mervyn's sister."

Mervyn, Iris thought more or less every time she received a letter from him, was the complete antithesis of Josephine. Perhaps that was why, when he had asked her to go to a concert with him one evening, her life had begun to fill up again. He was the other side of the coin which had Josephine's confident head on it. He was a man who looked as if his life had been one long flinch: from a father who had had no time for children, and who certainly hadn't wanted a son like Mervyn (he had just about managed to tolerate his daughter) and from a mother who, although she loved him, admitted cheerfully that she didn't understand him, and didn't really try to. She would have made a good mother of sons, but not a son like Mervyn. Poor Mervyn... She really ought to stop saying that. By the time she had got to know him the flinch had settled down to a sort of tentativeness, as if he always expected the answer "no". Perhaps Josephine was right when she said it was inevitable that he should have been a teacher. Somehow, for all his talent (and he was talented, very talented) he lacked the impetus necessary to do more with it than teach. She had also said (less than kindly, in Iris's view) that it was equally inevitable that he should have chosen a girls' school to teach in, and that from the all-female staff Iris was the one to whom he was attracted. Iris knew what she meant in a way: Mervyn was fond of her, as fond of her as she was of him, but attraction was definitely too strong a word for it. Attraction, when it did come, came powerfully and suddenly and unexpectedly, and Josephine had taken a good deal of convincing, in fact Iris wasn't altogether certain she was convinced even now.

One thing that couldn't be denied, though, was that with the advent of Mervyn, life in Melbourne was well on the way to recovering some of its former gloss. Despite his apparent reclusiveness, he had a lot of friends, and when she looked back on that time it was a pleasantly blurry mixture of picnics and concerts and theatre-going and barbecues, with the occasional trip to Sydney thrown in; and the absence of Josephine was no longer a feature of it. She enjoyed doing things with Mervyn, he was comfortable to be with. It would have been nice to have been in love with him, but she wasn't. When she thought about it, she wondered if Nick had cured her of love and, if he had, whether she ought to be grateful.

The weekends and holidays in Melbourne which Josephine had so confidently predicted when announcing her imminent departure for Broken Hill had only rarely materialised. "You could count them on the *thumbs* of one hand!" had been Iris's comment. Nor were her letters and postcards much more numerous. She telephoned from time to time - brief, friendly, business-like calls to ask Iris how she was, and how the flat was, and the car, and if there were any problems and, in answer to Iris's enquiries, told her that life was fine, and the work was interesting and, on one occasion, that she had taken up gliding and, on another, that she was thinking of learning to fly, and that was virtually all the communication there had been from her. Iris had written to her - and continued to write to her - regularly, but she seldom received a reply, and Josephine's life remained as unknown as it had been when she first moved away. It came, therefore, as something of a shock when she rang up one Sunday morning to suggest that Iris (and Mervyn too, if he wanted to) might like to go up to Broken Hill to stay with her for a few days and see an English ballet company which was due to visit there in a couple of weeks. Iris mentioned it to Mervyn almost hesitantly.

"You don't have to go and stay with her if you don't want to. We could always see them when they come to Melbourne. I'm sure we'd still be able to get tickets."

But Mervyn had been rather taken with the idea. "The 'Sleeping Beauty' in Broken Hill? It's such a marvellous contradiction. It's irresistible! Besides, I've never been to the ballet."

"Really? Why ever not? Don't you like it?"

"Never thought about it. Just a left-over bit of good old Aussie chauvinism, I guess," and he went on in a mile-wide accent totally unlike his own, "watching all those fairies prancing about!"

Iris was pleased. She hoped that it might prove to be a happy opportunity for Josephine to see Mervyn at his best and maybe get to know him better. They had met briefly on one of Josephine's visits, but it had not been a particularly enjoyable experience in spite of Iris's efforts to show each of them off well to the other. Josephine had seemed to take a delight in baiting him, almost savagely, almost (Iris felt) as if she had hated him; but when she tackled her with it Josephine had shrugged it off with an airy "Oh, Merv's ok... for a mother's boy!"

"Why were you so horrid to him, then?"

"I wasn't horrid to him. I treated him like a brother."

Chapter 4

It was one of the hottest weeks of that year, with temperatures in Melbourne well over the 100 degree mark by day, and almost as hot at night. In Broken Hill it was even hotter, nor was the hall where the company was to perform rendered appreciably cooler by the whirring of dozens of electric fans. Iris had half expected the performance to be cancelled, but dancers, they discovered, were made of sterner stuff, and for two and a half hours the heat was eclipsed, intermittently at least, by the spectacle of ethereal creatures leaping and gliding and pirouetting effortlessly - which illusion was sustainable as long as one didn't look through the binoculars thoughtfully provided by Josephine. Through the binoculars, muscles could be observed, bunching and releasing, and tendons like steel wires, and knuckles, and hands gripping, and enough sweat to drown in. The dancers didn't just glow, they streamed - drops of sweat flying from them in all directions. Iris let Josephine have the monopoly of the binoculars. Mervyn was sitting in his shirt sleeves giving, according to Josephine, a good imitation of someone who had just emerged from a Turkish bath, but looking to Iris as if the spell being enacted on the stage had somehow floated off like dry ice, enveloping him completely. He sat in a cocoon of enchantment akin to shock, not speaking, hardly applauding (nor was that out of deference to the heat), totally entranced. If ever he spoke of it afterwards it was in the words and special rapt voice she might have expected from St. Paul after he had reached Damascus. The hectic fanning of programmes during the interval left him undisturbed. Even the call for a doctor which took Josephine hurrying from her seat to somewhere behind the faded blue velvet curtains failed to rouse him.

After the performance they learned that one of the dancers had twisted her knee. "I'm afraid she'll be out for the rest of the tour," Josephine informed them. "It's a shame. She's a nice kid."

"She'll be all right, will she? I mean, it won't mean the end of her career?"

"Good Lord, no. She's got it strapped up. All she needs now is rest and then some physio. She may need surgery later, but I think she'll make it without. God, I thought we worked hard, but those kids... whew! Classes and rehearsals even when they're on tour, Albina says. No wonder they're fit."

Josephine had taken the young Albina under her wing, which meant in effect that Iris and Mervyn had taken her under their collective wing while Josephine was at work. Because her injury had occurred early on in the tour, it had been decided to send her home as soon as possible so that she could have treatment there. Iris thought it would be nice if they were to take her back with them to Melbourne to spend a few days seeing some of the sights before returning to England.

"There's precious little for her to see here, that's for sure," Mervyn had agreed with her.

"And we're too far from Alice or Ayers Rock or anywhere like that," Iris added for good measure.

Josephine pooh-poohed the plan. Mervyn, she said, drove like a spinster: "Albina'll have a hellish journey. You'll never make it in a day. More like two, if at all, and all for the sake of some boring old war memorial. She'll be better off staying here a bit longer and then flying down... or getting the train."

"Jo," Iris had soothed, "I know it's a long journey, but it won't necessarily be the War Memorial. She hasn't seen a koala or a duck-billed platypus... or even a kangaroo, come to that." She wasn't entirely sure about the kangaroo. "Mervyn thought we might take a picnic to Healesville. We'll look after her, I promise. Why don't you take a couple of days off and come down with us?" Iris thought it unlikely that she would be able to, but it had the desired effect. Josephine was mollified.

They had set out very early the following morning when it was still dark - there wouldn't be anything of note to see in the country through which they were to travel but, as it turned out, Albina was enraptured by everything: a solitary wind-pump had her marvelling at the space and loneliness of it all; the sight of a deserted homestead or a group of dead gum trees bleached to silvered whiteness like ghost trees on an ancient battlefield brought tears to her eyes, and more than once they heard her murmur: "those poor, poor people."

Mervyn became quite voluble, and discoursed at some length on the use of corrugated iron in farm building and early Australian architecture in general, and Albina listened, all eyes and attentiveness. She contrasted the bone-white land with the greenness of England, and wondered if anyone could ever have hoped to create another England there. It was a wonder, they all agreed. And, gradually, mile upon mile of the same terrain slowed the conversation to a trickle which, as the sun rose higher in the sky, dried up completely.

Mervyn wanted to talk, Iris could tell by the one or two false starts which he converted into a cough, and by the glances he kept directing towards Albina; but the only way he seemed able to express himself was by pressing his foot harder on the accelerator. A clump of trees whipped past them faster than the thought that turned her eyes involuntarily towards the speedometer. "Mervyn!" She prodded his shoulder, her voice a high-pitched squeak, "you're doing *ninety*!"

"Am I?" He laughed a most un-Mervyn-like laugh, and raised his foot a little: the car slowed down, although not quite enough to reassure her.

"Tell me about Jo. How long have you known her?" Albina's eyes, which were the nearest thing to violet that Iris had ever seen, were looking enquiringly at her. One hand lay lightly across the other on the back of the seat, and her body was curved in a half-spiral. Even on the front seat of a Holden, with her leg heavily bandaged, Albina could not help being graceful. It was her fortunate lot, Iris decided, to captivate everyone she met, and not by artifice either, she was entirely unaware of the effect she had on people. Even Josephine, who was not easily charmed, had been charmed by her, and as for Mervyn... well... she had only to look at the way he was driving... like a spinster, indeed! Jo should see him *now*! Hastily she invoked the patron saint of travellers in danger. Albina, however, seemed to be oblivious to everything that was going on round her. She was speaking again. "She's like Queen Christina. I see her at the prow of a ship with her hair streaming in the wind, sailing into the unknown."

"It's funny you should say that. That's how I first

saw her. Well, not in the prow exactly, but on deck... on the ship coming here. She was standing beside me when we set sail. She must have been the only person not crying."

"Has she ever been married?"

Iris shook her head. "I believe she was once engaged... sort of."

"Really?" Mervyn sounded surprised. "Who to?"

Iris ignored his "what poor schmuck?" tone of voice. "Back home when she was in practice with her father. I believe there was some sort of understanding between her and John, the other doctor in the practice, but whether it amounted to an engagement..." Iris shrugged, "anyway, it all ended when she came out here, I suppose. She always has plenty of men friends."

"Why did she come here?"

"She needed a change, or so she says. I don't know. I think maybe, after a time, she really does need a change of scene... it's like something that builds up in her blood: she has to be on the move again. She's been everywhere, really tough stuff, not just trips to Europe... South America... up the Amazon - or is it down the Amazon? Terra del Fuego... Africa... I don't think she's been to India but it's only a matter of time. I suppose she likes a challenge."

"I can't imagine her married," Mervyn interposed, without irony this time, "she's far too independent."

"Too bossy, you mean?" Josephine was certainly bossy with Mervyn. "Did I tell you she has four brothers?"

"Has she?" Albina's eyes opened wider. "I wish I had brothers... even one would be nice."

"Do you have any sisters?"

"No, nothing. It's just me. Lucky Jo… I wish I was like her."

Mervyn's eyes swerved off the road in his amazement, and the car swerved with them. Iris couldn't prevent another squeak. He brought it under control again.

"Wouldn't you say, Iris," he asked seriously, "that she… Albina… is the nearest thing to perfection you've ever seen?"

"Mmm." Iris nodded her head and glanced at her normally reticent friend who had suddenly applied himself to the business of driving, with great concentration. Albina's cheeks, she noticed, had turned quite pink.

Mervyn wanted to know how she had come to be a dancer.

"My parents took me to see Markova dance when I was little. I'd never seen anything like it. I'd been to pantomimes and things like that, but this wasn't like dancing at all. It was like…" she looked away out of the car at the horizon, "like all the fairy tales rolled into one." She smiled. "I was very young. I couldn't believe she was real. I did meet her once, you know, when I was a student, and even then I didn't really believe she was real. Have you ever seen her feet? A dancer's feet are all knobby and ugly, but hers aren't. They're slender and… supple, like beautiful hands. I've never seen anything so beautiful. It's my dream to be like her."

"What about Fonteyn? Or Beryl Grey? Or Ulanova… what about her?"

Albina laughed. "Of course, any dancer would like to be like any of them, but Markova is my ideal.

So ethereal and..." she paused, "so strong." Her face glowed.

"What about other things? What about..?"

"Yes," Mervyn interrupted, "what about boyfriends? Haven't you got a boyfriend?"

She had never mentioned anyone other than her parents and Madame and members of the company.

"Oh no, nothing like that. I don't see how anyone can be married, or anything like that, and be a dancer at the same time." She frowned slightly: "You would have to skimp on one or the other. I couldn't do that."

"My word, you are a serious young woman." Mervyn's smile was gentle. "You don't think there's something a bit..." he paused for a moment, "unnatural about such dedication?"

"Oh no." The eyes were wide, the face innocent and ecstatic. However, Albina was not interested in talking about herself, she wanted to learn as much as she could about Josephine, and Iris was entertained by the turns and twists of the conversation as she and Mervyn manoeuvred it to suit their own particular wishes, and more particularly entertained by Mervyn because he was trying to please Albina and get his own way at the same time.

"You know," Mervyn said to Iris two days later, after they had been to Moorabbin to see Albina off, "if she wasn't a dancer, she'd be a nun. Or St. Joan."

"Oh, not St. Joan, surely? St. Joan's far too militant."

"Can't you see her being burned at the stake for her faith?"

"Ye-es. But if we're thinking of saints, I'd say St.

Theresa is more her line... St. Theresa of Lisieux."

But Mervyn didn't agree with her. "Oh no. Much too namby pamby." Iris laughed. "With her Little Way. No... our Albina's is a bright, clear, burning way... straight to God." He stopped, embarrassed, Iris could tell, by his own eloquence.

When she spoke again, her voice was sad: "But, you know, you're right about the dedication." She had gone into the spare bedroom before they set out for the airport, to make sure that Albina hadn't left anything behind, and had found a note tucked in the frame of the mirror. Thinking it might be something important, she had read it. It said; "I must not fail."

Later, when she tidied the room, she had found several more scraps of paper screwed up in the waste paper basket. She felt a niggle of guilt at reading them, but couldn't help herself. One said: "will power", and another: "pain makes perfect", and yet another vowed quite simply: "I will."

In the years afterwards, Iris remembered them sometimes, and wished that she could have felt uplifted. But what she wished most of all was that she had never seen them.

Chapter 5

Josephine was huddled on the half-landing two-thirds of the way up the stairs with Iris sitting a step or two below her. It had taken them hours to get there, Iris was not sure just how many and she wasn't keen to find out, all she knew was that it had taken them far longer than she could possibly have imagined. Of course, they had already been tired before they had begun their ascent, so tired that even a fortifying cup of tea and several rounds of toast and honey had only been able to fuel them for the first three or four stairs. After that Josephine's arms had given out and Iris had had to hoist her bodily up each step, with increasingly frequent stops for rest.

"I want to go to the lav."

"Oh Jo." Perhaps if she ignored her she would forget about it.

"*Iris!*"

There was no ignoring that! "Can you hang on till we get upstairs? It's only six more to go."

"I don't think so. I know it's only six more."

"Jo... let me call Margery. Please? We could have you tucked up in bed in a trice if you'd only let me."

"I absolutely forbid it. Think of something else."

"Oh, you're impossible! I'm going to fetch her." Iris stood up.

"If you do, I... I'll throw myself down the stairs!"

"You wouldn't."

"Try me." She leaned towards the top stair. Iris pushed her back sharply.

"All right. All right. I'll get a bowl from the

bathroom."

"I'm not doing anything in a plastic bowl."

"Then you'll just have to hang on. No... wait." She edged past Josephine, "I've a better idea." She hurried up the stairs and along the landing to Josephine's bedroom. The long-handled hook for opening the trap-door into the loft was in the corner by the wardrobe. She seized it and went back to the landing. For once she managed to snare the ring at the first try. She pulled, and pulled again more forcefully. The aluminium ladder swung down with the controlled ease which always delighted her. Quickly, she climbed up, and then wasted several seconds groping in the darkness for the light switch. She looked round her. It was so tempting to let oneself be side-tracked by almost anything up there, especially on a day when memory was running riot - disused possibilities lay everywhere: a rocking chair and an old rocking horse, chipped and maneless, a print of Melbourne given to Val by Marco, and consigned to the loft after she fell out of love with him, two camp-beds and several preserving pans (how did they come to have so many?) all jostled for her attention. There were ancient medical books belonging to Josephine's father; there were suitcases and trunks and, lying on one of them, the box of Scrabble, faded and peeling along its edges, which had seen a brief revival of interest when Val was in her teens; there was a solar topee (she couldn't somehow envisage Josephine wearing it, so who it belonged to was a puzzle) and a wind-up gramophone and somewhere, she knew, there was a willow-patterned chamber-pot. It was just a matter of finding it. She had an idea it might be in one of several tea-chests, along with other odds and ends of china garnered over the years, but which one? The first was full of old 78 gramophone records, and although the next one looked more promising it yielded only a photograph album, a pair of riding boots, an assortment of shoes, not all in pairs and many of which Iris didn't recognise, a mackintosh riding-cape, stiff and brittle in its folds as old brown cardboard, and two brass candlesticks covered in verdigris. She had been right about the tea-chests though, and the third one surrendered the precious pot without the need for any further rummaging. She hurried back to the ladder with it, only pausing, in a moment of inquisitiveness impossible to resist, to pick up the photograph album before switching off the light.

A loose snapshot fluttered down the steps ahead of her. After she had returned the ladder to its roost and checked that the trap-door was closed properly, she stooped to retrieve it. It was a picture of Val as a little girl. Iris remembered the black coat with the velvet collar and wondered why anyone would have bothered to take a picture of her in it.

When she got back to her she found Josephine crying with all the abandonment of a baby. Josephine never cried. Not since she was a child, if she was to be believed. She hadn't cried at Albina's funeral or at Ruth's and Gerald's, and Iris guessed that she probably hadn't even shed a tear for her father - grieved for him perhaps, in her own way, but without tears.

"Jo, dear, what on earth's the matter?"

"You were gone so long."

Triumphantly, Iris held out the chamber-pot, but it

seemed only to make matters worse. Nor was she able to elicit what the trouble was, Josephine being by now so immersed in grief as to render everything she said unintelligible. After a minute or so of Iris coaxing and trying to dry her eyes for her, and having her hand pushed away, Josephine managed to blurt out that nothing she wanted to work did, and that only those organs she'd rather forget about betrayed her. Unable to hold on any longer, she had shit herself, she said, and wailed again.

Iris's head cleared. The crowd of memories vanished. All her old Mother Iris instincts took over, ousting the utter weariness which had been sapping her mind as well as her body. Up and down the stairs, she went, collecting buckets and Dettol and warm water and plenty of towels and some bin-liners. In what seemed no time at all, she had managed to slip one of these under Josephine and had peeled off the malodorous lower garments and dumped them in a bucket of disinfectant. Her actions were quick and sure and business-like, blotting out thought. She wiped off most of the excrement with cotton wool and baby oil and then, using some old soft pieces of towelling, washed her until she was satisfied that every crinkled fold of skin was clean. That done, she eased Josephine over on to her side so that she could replace the bin-liner with a fresh one; she covered it with a towel and proceeded gently and firmly to press and pat her until she was completely dry. The operation was finished off with a flourish of talcum powder.

She fetched pyjamas and a sweater and socks and Josephine's winter dressing-gown from her room, and went to the bathroom to refill the bowl of warm water before kneeling down beside her again to wash the rest of her. She felt oddly detached from her actions, oddly peaceful. There was no disgust at what had happened, nor any distaste with what she was doing. If she was aware of anything at all, it was of a mild surprise at the suspension of her own fastidiousness. It was only when she had finished and was taking the buckets and the paraphernalia of washing back to the kitchen, that she realised there were tears running down her cheeks. She put the soiled garments and towels into the washing-machine and switched it on. The tears continued, but she didn't bother to check them. When they stopped there was nothing - no emotion, nothing except stillness, and a certain inexplicable sense of expectancy.

Chapter 6

"I notice there's been less talk of dying since we've been on the move."

"Oh, I'm dying all right."

"No more than any of us are. What made you think it in the first place, for goodness' sake?"

"I don't know. Mortality, I guess."

"Mortality?"

"Yes."

"Everyone's mortal."

"I wasn't. Not till recently. It happened quite suddenly: I was immortal... and then... bingo! I think it was when I felt guilty at not giving up my seat for someone on the bus the last time I was in London... she must have been all of sixty-five, poor old girl. Suddenly, I knew I wasn't immortal any more."

"I've known it for years... since I was about forty-five... most people do."

"Well, I didn't. Don't ask me why. God knows, doctors know more about mortality than most... I just didn't think it applied to me. Mortality only happens to other people. You know... like not getting away with murder."

Iris laughed. "Oh, I always thought it was a bit like the menopause... something that came on you at a certain time of life."

"Not with me, it didn't. *Imm*ortal," she emphasised the first syllable, "that's what I was. I was beginning to feel like Methuselah." Iris's eyebrows rose enquiringly. "The prospect of living for ever is appalling, don't you think?"

"I wouldn't know. I would have thought the thing about believing you're immortal is that you don't actually *think* it at all, you just are. And then, one day, you know you aren't." She smiled. "You're right... it must be quite a relief."

"It was most peculiar..." Josephine was talking to herself rather than to Iris, "I wasn't ill... I just had the feeling that nothing was working the way it used to, like someone was pointing the bone at me." She glanced upwards and nodded. "It was as if I could have stopped it all myself... it would have needed the merest effort of will. I could feel my pulse... hear my heart beating... borborigmi and all that... but running down. And another thing..." she looked at Iris accusingly, "the world has retreated."

"How do you mean, retreated?"

"Oh, Iris," she sighed.

In the silence that followed Iris wondered if that was it, and Josephine and talk and life had finally ceased.

"You know how, on a very hot day, sometimes everything seems remote? All the sounds are far away, and there's a sort of haze of silence over everything?" Iris nodded. "Well, it's a bit like that, except that the silence is in *me*, radiating out."

"Perhaps you're not dying at all. The tides of the body don't just stop because you want them to. Perhaps it's something quite different."

"Like what, for instance?" The old haughty look was back.

"Oh, I don't know. Like not eating enough and being light-headed. You haven't eaten properly for days. You haven't eaten *anything*."

"No, it's nothing like that. I'd recognise that.

This is something quite different."

"Perhaps you're diabetic."

The scorn in Josephine's expression would, momentarily at least, have shrivelled Iris before this day. But today she had pushed and pulled and heaved and humped and hauled her up to the half-landing rather like a dung-beetle manoeuvring its out-sized burden up a bumpy slope. "Just like a dung-beetle, in fact." She didn't realise that she had spoken out loud until Josephine snapped: "What are you rambling on about, Iris?" And she was silent again.

"I've always felt I had a grip on life..." Josephine's voice sounded plaintive, "now it's slipping... running away through my fingers."

"Poor Jo." Iris stroked her cheek. It was only later, when she was lying in bed, too exhausted, it seemed, for sleep, that she marvelled at the moderateness of Josephine's "Don't you 'poor Jo' me. Get me to bed."

"You'll have to wait till the morning..." Josephine opened her mouth, "if you don't want me to fetch Margery. I know it's not all that comfortable here, but I really am worn out. I don't think I can do any more today without help."

"I'll die here, like as not."

"No you won't. I won't let you. Now... I'm just going to fetch an eiderdown for you, and then you can have a drop of soup and," she was already on her feet, "anything else you fancy."

She gathered up the eiderdown from Josephine's bed, and a duvet from the spare room, and several pillows which she arranged under and round her, cushioning her back and buttocks and elbows, before wrapping her in the duvet.

"I don't think you'll need the eiderdown, but I've brought it just in case." She draped it over the newell post at the top of the stairs. Josephine was looking pink and relaxed and clean, and Iris descended with a lighter step than she had had all day. As she passed the sitting-room, the bracket clock chimed the half hour and she glanced at her watch. It was half past eight. "Heavens!"

She called out: "I'm just going to phone Val. Is there anything you want me to say?"

"Not specially. Tell her what you like."

Val was worried, but hadn't telephoned in case Iris was busy. She was pleased with her day's work, she said, and asked how Jo was.

"It's hard to tell. She's not ill exactly... not what *you'd* call ill... but she's..." Iris searched for a word that would be honest but unworrying, "different." That would have to do.

"I'll come home tomorrow. My exam's in the afternoon. I'll drive down after that."

"Thank you, darling. How's Edwin doing?"

"Oh, fine. He's actually enjoying it all, believe it or not."

"Gracious." Iris could think of nothing more to say. "Good luck tomorrow. Love to Edwin. Jo sends love." As she replaced the receiver, she noticed her duster lying where she had left it on the mantelpiece in the morning; she retrieved it with a mild click-click of her tongue and tossed it into the broom cupboard as she passed.

Josephine was hungry and needed no persuading to take a little chicken broth with vegetables sliced up in it. She had finished it, as well as the bread and butter, by the time Iris put a bowl of fruit beside her and sat down on the stair below.

"How do you feel?"

"All right... pretty much the same... I don't know. For God's sake stop nagging."

Iris waited for the grumpy expression to clear. "I found a photo album in the loft. Do you want to have a look? I've no idea what's in it."

"Ok."

"You're sure you're not too tired?" Josephine frowned again. "I'll get it."

Most of the dust had been rubbed off in its journey down from the loft, and now she gave it a perfunctory wipe over with her apron before slapping the covers together. Once again the loose snapshot fluttered out and she picked it up. All the family photograph albums were in Val's room; there was a whole row of them at the bottom of one of the book-cases. It was Val who, once she was of an age to accompany Josephine on some of her expeditions, had been the photographer. Josephine had never needed anything to remind her of her travels. Her journeyings were inspired as much by the needs of the spirit as by love of travel itself, and she had certainly had no need of photographs. It was the very unaccountability of this old album that intrigued Iris. She saw now that there were some photographs in it she had never seen before, and she thought she had seen them all. There were two or three which she remembered of a picnic by the sea when Val had first come to live with them, and several of an unknown man on horseback.

"Who is that?"

Josephine turned to the next page and the next, skimming past snapshots, some black and white, some in colour, with the speed of a what-the-butler-saw machine. Iris thought she recognised Josephine's father among them, and some of Marco. The flickering pages slowed down and stopped finally at a portrait of Albina in her wedding dress. On the page facing it were two smaller pictures, one of Albina leaving the church on the arm of her new husband (Josephine had been the photographer on that occasion - she had slipped out of the church ahead of the bride and groom so that she could "snap them up before the professionals get at them" - Iris smiled at the surprised look on their faces) and another of them cutting the cake.

"I remember," she ventured, "reading a review of Moira Shearer dancing Cinderella: it said she shimmered with happiness."

"Doesn't sound like any review I've ever read."

"It did though. Shimmered with happiness. Albina shimmered on her wedding day. It's a bit of a cliché to talk about radiance, isn't it? But she was radiant. I can see her in the church now. Like a thousand diamonds... or was it dewdrops? Anyway, that's what it said. I remember thinking of it at the time."

Josephine laughed, not unkindly. "I worry about you sometimes, Iris."

"She went on a retreat, did you know that? Before she got married."

"It doesn't surprise me. After all, she was convent educated."

Iris was doubtful about the logic of that. She turned the page to a snapshot of Val trying on her bridesmaid's dress. She had protested at having her picture taken and was making a silly face, but in a second picture Josephine had managed to catch her

57

off-guard and she was looking really quite pretty. "Ah, bless her." Iris turned the page back again and looked once more at Albina.

"I wondered where this had got to. She was a lovely girl, wasn't she? Unusually lovely really... not just conventionally pretty... those violet eyes."

"Nobody has violet eyes."

"She did."

"A trick of the light... or make-up. Her eyes were grey."

"They looked violet to me. Mervyn always said they were violet." Iris ignored the snort. "I remember him saying something about it after we'd driven her back to Melbourne that time, and saying about her being not quite of this world. Do you remember... we saw her as the Lilac Fairy... back in London?"

"Violet eyes... there you are, you see! You're getting them mixed up with that."

"And in Giselle... do you remember?"

"Mmm... no brains."

"Jo!"

"It's true. Talented, I grant you... extremely talented... but not a lot in the way of cerebral convolutions."

"She must have had *some* brains to be a dancer, surely?"

"Not really. With her it was purely instinctive. She had a perfect dancer's body, of course, and innate musical sense, plus a sort of intuitive ability to interpret a role. She couldn't have told you how she did it. Barely a hundred pence in the pound."

"You're very cruel sometimes, Jo."

"Rubbish."

"Then why were you so unkind to her when she was so ill?"

"I wasn't unkind. I did everything I could. You know that. I spent *hours* with her."

"I know you did. It wasn't that."

"I don't know what else I could have done."

"You never said a kind word to her in all that time."

"How do you know?"

"Her father told me. 'No word of comfort... never one.' That's what he said."

"She didn't want comfort... not from me."

"Maybe he wanted it for her, poor man. Maybe he wanted it for himself."

"H'm." Josephine shrugged slightly. "I couldn't forgive her. She was such a saint. God, I can see her now... lying there... dying perfectly." She made a growling sound in her throat.

Iris closed her eyes. She could picture Albina's home quite clearly: pretty as a Sanderson print... prettier if that were possible. Pretty and elegant and comfortable as well. Everything had its place, and when the children were born - a boy (Michael, after his father) followed two years later by a girl (Josephine, after her godmother) they had their places too. Albina, who had gone on a retreat in order to prepare for marriage, had applied herself to being a wife and mother with the same simple, unquestioning single-mindedness that she had previously lavished on dancing, and with similar success.

"It was her last vocation."

"What d'you mean?"

"Albina needed a vocation... don't you think? First of all it was dancing... then marriage - you

59

said yourself how idyllic that was... more than once."

"Ugh!" Josephine grimaced. "Nauseating. That beautiful home, and Michael adoring Albina, and Albina adoring Michael, and their adored children adoring them." She shuddered. "Ugh... it made you want to bite into a whole lemon!"

"She really worked at it. I suppose she worked at everything she did. It all had to be perfect... was perfect... a labour of love."

"Don't go on about it, Iris."

"And then, when she was ill... when she knew... the last vocation of all."

"Damn Albina!"

"Jo!"

"We-ell... look at her... forcing memory on us. I don't *want* to remember."

"Jo," Iris remonstrated again.

"I just don't think we need to nourish ourselves with memories the way you seem to. It's not healthy."

"There's nothing unhealthy about it at all. It's natural."

Josephine was adamant. "Don't talk about her, Iris... it still makes me mad."

Iris turned the pages. "You were always a bit like that, you know, even with ordinary illness."

"What d'you mean, '*ordinary* illness'? What was I like?"

"Like when Val had measles. You never went near her."

"I did."

"Not till she was on the mend."

"Well... you were always so secretive."

"Secretive?"

"Yes. I only ever knew she was ill when I saw you sneaking into her room with a bottle of jollop hidden behind your back."

"Jo," Iris couldn't help laughing, "you know you never went anywhere near her... and you're her *aunt*!"

"We-ell... you were so good at doing it all. I'd only have got in the way."

"Oh, Jo... you're impossible." Iris turned back a page. "I don't remember that one. Where is it?" It was a picture of a small, walled garden, or as much of the garden as could be glimpsed through an archway in the stone wall. The person taking the photograph had been in shadow, but the garden was luminous with sunlight. Iris could see part of a weathered wooden seat, and flag-stones with what looked like herbs growing up through the cracks between them. There was something old and long-established about it, even the peach tree growing against the wall behind the seat, and the roses, had been there a long time. You could feel the warmth, smell the fragrance almost. There was no-one there, no-one you could see, and yet Iris had the feeling of a presence, of someone sitting... perhaps on that part of the seat that was hidden from view. She was being fanciful, she knew. She turned back a few more pages. "Who is that?"

Josephine said nothing.

"Do I know him?"

When she replied, her tone was off-hand: "Just a chap I met when I was in the Service." She closed the album and smoothed her hand over the cover. "We had a call to a cattle station in the outback... one of the hands had come off his horse and been crushed during mustering. It turned out to be his son. Didn't I tell you about him?"

"I don't think so. You know perfectly well you didn't. Anyway, you didn't write all that often... I don't think I had more than half a dozen letters from you in seven years."

"Ed. Edward James Murray. Ed Murray... same as Val's chum... funny, that. Nice man." She frowned. "I telephoned quite often."

"You never mentioned any Ed Murray. Anyway, Val's young man is Edwin. When you did write it was mostly stuff about other doctors and people in Broken Hill. Or gliding. That was one of your best... practically a manual... I could have taken up gliding without an instructor after your letter on *that* subject."

"Ah... gliding..." Josephine leaned back and closed her eyes.

Iris thought she remembered Josephine saying something about being off up to Ed's place for a few days. "You may have mentioned him once... I thought he must be another doctor... or one of the pilots. Tell me about him."

Josephine opened the album and looked at the photograph of him before closing it once more. "He was a great guy. He had a marvellous, beat-up old face. Not that old, really, but weather-beaten... battered... you can't see it properly in those snaps. And four sons... they all lived out there in that God-forsaken place, miles from anywhere. His grandfather had gone out there from Scotland way back in the eighteen hundreds. The boys all had Scottish names: Doug... Douglas, Robert, James, Andrew. He was quite proud of his ancestry. He had the bluest eyes, like forget-me-nots, and..." she paused, "thighs like tree trunks, like..." she laughed a soft, exultant laugh, "like a Suffolk Punch. I nearly married him."

"He was a widower, then?" Josephine nodded. "Why didn't you?"

"It would have been a disaster. For both of us. He was too nice a bloke to do that to... very male-ish, as Albina used to say... an honest-to-God man." She shook her head. "It would never have worked."

She opened the album again and leafed through the pages, stopping every now and then to look at a particular photograph. "I oughtn't to say his place was God-forsaken. It was miles... hundreds of miles... from anywhere, but it was beautiful... not so much God-forsaken as God's own country really. Red... and beautiful... and very, very old." Her eye-lids drooped. "You say Dorset gives you a feeling of antiquity..."

"Dorset? Yes... pre history."

"This was more ancient than that... more..." she paused, "timeless. Before time was..." she opened her eyes, "you know?"

"The dream time."

"I suppose...yes. We used to ride out before dawn, checking fences. I spent a week with him doing that once... I never got tired of it. You can see the country from a glider all right, but you can't get the *feel* of it. How can you when you're up there floating about on thermals? Horseback's the thing... making camp at night..." her voice trailed away.

"That's you there, isn't it?" Iris pointed to two people in jeans and checked shirts, both on horseback.

Josephine smiled. "I'd forgotten that one. That

was Ed's shirt and one of the boys' hats… Doug's, I think. Suits me, doesn't it?"

"You look beaut." She did too, and they laughed, contented laughter subsiding gently into amiable silence. Josephine yawned. "Come on. You ought to get some sleep. Do you want me to stay here with you?"

"No, I'll be all right. You must go to bed. You must be whacked."

There was one more journey down the stairs to fetch the plank from the chair in the sitting-room. Iris wedged it between the banisters across the top of the stairs. "We don't want you rolling over in the night." She shivered slightly and went up to the bathroom.

"I've brought you your toothbrush and things." She set down a bowl of water and a towel in the corner of the half-landing, with the tooth mug and brush and tooth-paste beside them.

"You know," Josephine's voice was dreamy, "when I was little I used to wish for a djinn or afreet to carry me off to bed with my teeth cleaned and my hair brushed."

"A djinn or afreet would come in very handy right now."

Josephine chuckled and mumbled something inaudible and, still murmuring, sank deeper into the duvet nest.

"Jo?"

"Mmm?"

"If she didn't want comforting, what did she want?"

"Oh…" Josephine opened her eyes a little and squinted at a horizon beyond the staircase while she pondered. "Someone to travel with part of the way, I guess." Her eyes closed again.

Iris continued to sit by her. She was conscious more of a sense of achievement than of any definite thought. Once or twice her eyes closed and, before she should doze off altogether, she roused herself and gathered up Josephine's washing things, slowly carrying them up the half dozen stairs to the bathroom. She had been tempted to go straight to bed, but Iris had never once in all her life gone to bed without cleaning her teeth, so now she squeezed out her tooth-brush length of tooth-paste and watched her reflection brushing up and down methodically and rhythmically behind and round the back teeth, then down over the upper teeth, as she had been taught, and up over the lower ones. She was proud of her teeth. Other bits of her told the truth about her age: her skin, being fair, was particularly candid - indeed, had there been no skull to support it, it would have flopped like a spent and colourless balloon; there were unflattering hollows, too, round her eyes and below her cheekbones and running down each side of her mouth. She was reminded, not for the first time, of her grandmother who, on a day when she had decided to "give her face a rest" by not dusting her cheeks with the hare's foot dipped in the little pot of rouge on her dressing-table, had been greeted by a neighbour with the words: "Oh, Missus, you do look washed out!" After which, she had never given her face a rest again. On a good day Iris knew that she still retained something of her former looks, but today the teeth received an extra brushing. Never mind, she thought, tomorrow must be easier. I'll get Jo to bed after breakfast, and Val should be home by seven at the latest. She'll talk some sense into her.

She left the light on in the bathroom, letting it shine through the open door on to the landing. Everything was quiet as she walked softly past the top of the stairs to her room. Here, too, she kept the door open and, without bothering to undress, lay down gratefully on her bed. She pulled the duvet up to her chest. Mervyn's letter crackled in her apron pocket; it had remained there along with the digestive biscuits she had picked up earlier, forgotten in the welter of the day's small adventures - even Josephine had failed to remember it - forgotten, or at any rate left to one side much as Mervyn himself had been left to one side once the young Valentina had arrived to occupy her days and thoughts. Mervyn, I'm sorry. Iris sat up and removed the biscuits - a bit crumbly now - and the crumpled airmail envelope before untying her apron and dropping it on the chair beside her bed. I shan't open it now. But, even as she thought it, she switched on her bedside light to scrutinise the small, neat hand-writing which had grown smaller and more tightly ravelled as Mervyn had grown older. Her spectacles were downstairs. The letter would have to wait after all. She switched off the light.

Chapter 7

Now that she was lying there with the faint glow from the bathroom light showing through the doorway, sleep - which had seemed so imminent when she had been sitting beside Josephine - was proving reluctant to take over. Errant sleep... she sighed and hoped that the rest would do her as much good. Her thoughts had disobligingly woken up, and a lively mix of memory and mortality and the day's activities effervesced in her brain. Ed Murray's thighs and Josephine's soft, deep, exultant, throaty, luxuriating laugh when she had spoken of them disturbed her in a way that she had not been disturbed for many a tranquil decade. She found that for all the immediacy of her memories, she could not remember Nick's thighs at all, much as she had loved him. She could remember Mervyn's thighs or, rather, she could remember his legs. They were surprisingly good for such a wispy man (Josephine's words) and even Josephine had been unable to find anything to disparage except, of course, that her surprise was disparagement enough.

What would have happened had she stayed in Melbourne? None of this, that was for sure. Once Mervyn had come into it, her life there had begun to develop a life of its own, and she had had less need of a Josephine. Before, it had always been Josephine who had had the ideas and plans, and Iris who had tagged along, their friendship most definitely not one between equals, but with Iris happy enough for it to be that way. With Mervyn, on the other hand, things were much more evenly balanced, neither of them quite complete on their own, but together forming a nice, compact, even fairly strong, unit. One evening, after a concert, he had asked her if she had ever thought of building her own house.

"What? What did you say?"

"Yes. Buying a block of land and building your own home. Have you ever thought of it?"

And she had laughed. "You must be joking. It takes money. Where would I find that sort of money? In another ten years maybe."

"Would you consider coming in with me?"

Marriage was not what she had expected or wanted from Mervyn, or indeed from anyone any more, and she was relieved when he clearly deemed it necessary - or perhaps polite - to add: "I am not asking you to marry me… and I'm not," he had smiled rather self-consciously, "suggesting anything irregular. I hope you understand."

"What about the school?"

"What about the school? It's none of their business, is it? And if it was, there would be nothing reprehensible in it."

"No… nothing reprehensible!" she teased him. He used words she didn't hear every day, not even from fellow members of staff.

"What about your mother?"

"She'd be glad to get rid of me. It's a drag for her having me around all the time. She'll be able to please herself, get spliced again if she wants to. I bet there's some sprightly old widower just dying to get his hands on her. She's a fine-looking woman. And she likes you."

Iris smiled. "It's very tempting."

It hadn't taken her long to come to a decision and,

at the same time, to decide not to tell Josephine about it immediately. There would be opportunity enough for that when they had found a piece of land they liked and the negotiations had been completed and the building started. There really was no need to do anything about Josephine just yet.

From then on they had started to plan. They both fancied the idea of moving away from the centre of Melbourne, and many of their Sundays were spend looking at likely plots of land in the more distant suburbs east and west of the city, and even farther out in places which were not yet suburbs. In the end, travelling towards the Dandenongs, they picked on a site on sloping land in Vermont where the sound of a bell bird chiming in a blue wattle made up their minds for them.

"Beautiful," said Mervyn.

"Magical," Iris had agreed, and crossed her fingers that the bell bird would still be there when their house was completed.

And then, quite suddenly, everything had changed again. Josephine had descended from Broken Hill one Friday evening, like Nebuchadnezzar on the unsuspecting fold, with the words: "We're going home!"

Iris remembered asking her if she wanted a cup of tea, and remembered thinking at the same time what an idiotic thing to have said, while Josephine helped herself to a glass of whisky. She fluttered about, horribly aware that she was dithering, and sat down facing Josephine who immediately stood up.

"I can't just pull up and go."

"Why not? What's to keep you here?"

"I can't. I've bought a block of land."

"Sell it."

"With Mervyn."

"Are you two going to get hitched then?"

"No-o." Josephine striding about like that made Iris feel that she hadn't explained things at all well. "For mutual companionship and... and protection." It wasn't the word she meant, they weren't any of them the words she meant.

"What d'you need protection for? You're perfectly capable of looking after yourself. Of course, *Mervyn..!*"

"It was a figure of speech."

"More like a figure of fun living with dear old Merv."

"Certainly not! He's a dear friend. A good friend."

"Huh!"

"Anyway, what's made you change your mind all of a sudden? I haven't heard from you since Christmas."

"Oh, things..." Josephine said, with a sweep of her hand as if that explained everything. "I need a change."

"You can't keep uprooting yourself because you think you need a change every six or seven years. You'll never get anywhere."

"I'm not concerned with getting anywhere. I wouldn't have gone into medicine if I'd wanted to get anywhere. But life's got to be interesting, and that means change, and that means *now*. Stay in Melbourne if you want... shack up with dear old Merv... he's a nice enough bloke. But you'll have more fun with me, changes and all."

And that was that.

"Mervyn, I'm so sorry." Iris was repeating her introductory apologies now that she was coming to the end of what struck her as a singularly inept, not to say implausible, string of excuses.

"It's all right. Really. I understand."

"I know I don't really owe her anything exactly. It's just that I feel I do. Not nearly as much as I owe you." She glanced at him. "But she sort of saved my life, you know." How Josephine would have scoffed. "I'm sure she doesn't see it like that though."

"I know."

"And there's another thing, if I'm honest… and… and I don't expect you to understand because I don't suppose it's ever happened to you, and I don't really understand it myself…" tears came into her eyes, "she mentioned home. I had no idea what an emotive word that could be." She felt in her pockets for a handkerchief. "I thought she was happy with her life. I really thought she'd stay with the Service till she retired. She's always saying how much she loves the bush and everything. The job was tailor-made for her. I can't imagine what's happened to make her change her mind."

"Home, perhaps."

"Mmm… I don't think so somehow. You know her. Wouldn't you say home was wherever she was at the moment?"

"Possibly."

"I can't think of anyone else you could say that about, but I'm sure it's true of her. No. If it's anything other than pure whim…" crossness almost succeeded in stifling the guilt, "she's not going to let on. Change, she says. H'mm." She paused. "But home…" the word trailed away, rising slightly as it died. "It makes me feel like Mole in 'The Wind in the Willows'. You know?"

Mervyn nodded.

"Please forgive me."

"There's nothing to forgive. We're good mates, you and me. Without you I'd never have taken the step in the first place. I'll buy you out."

"Can you afford it?"

"I've fallen for the place... I can't *not* afford it. When it's built, you must come and see it. There's really nothing to apologise for." He smiled and shook his head emphatically. "Nothing to forgive."

I don't deserve such kindness, she remembered thinking. She may even have said it.

She lay there, shifting her position slightly. She never had been back to see it, she had never been back at all. Josephine had gone once with Val, and Mervyn had come to stay with them several times, but her life since then seemed to have changed so completely, and there had been so much that was new and absorbing to occupy every moment of it, that the thought of going, let alone the desire to go, had never arisen. Of course, she would have liked to have seen it, but she had Mervyn's photographs, and his letters. And how many letters there had been over the years, hundreds probably: brief letters full of news about their house - he always referred to it as their house - and about his life, and all the things he knew would interest her. Although by nature reticent, he could be surprisingly revealing at times. In a letter written soon after Albina's death, he had said: "I wish to God I didn't know she was dead, then she would still be alive." A veritable torrent of letters had issued from him at that time; he seemed to have written to everyone... to anyone who had known her. He had even written to Josephine.

"I don't know what he's writing to *me* for. What on earth does he expect *me* to say to him?"

"Perhaps he thinks you loved her as much as he did."

"He didn't love her. He's incapable of that sort of love. He's a-loving."

"That's not true, Jo."

"He hasn't got it in him."

"You didn't see him with her. You haven't read his letters. He adored her."

"Rubbish."

"Everyone did. You know they did. She had that effect on people. You loved her."

"Don't keep saying that."

And then, abruptly, all the letters had stopped. There had been nothing for more than a year.

"I have a feeling he's ill, that's why he hasn't written. He's ill." It was a euphemism for a darker fear, one which surfaced only when she was off her guard during the defenceless hours of the night.

Whatever Josephine might say, and whatever her reasons for having those opinions, Iris knew that she was wrong about Mervyn. As some people can divine water, so she had a sixth sense about love, the state of being in love, the depth and genuineness of it. Being cured of it herself, the gods, it seemed, had granted her the gift of seeing it in others, and she saw it in Mervyn. It wasn't fairy-tale love or Hollywood romantic, it was a graceful, courtly, chivalric, but none the less real, passion, and he could not have chosen a more ideal recipient. Only Josephine, like Carabosse uninvited at the christening, was wilfully uncomprehending.

"Ring him up then."

"I couldn't do that."

"Why not?"

"I don't know. I don't want to intrude."

"It wouldn't be intruding."

But Iris had waited, hoping, and trusting in her intuition, and she had been right to be patient.

Some years later in their correspondence, one or two letters mentioned a young student, Marco, who had come to lodge with him: nothing heavy, as Val used to say, just a mention here and there.

"Now it wouldn't surprise me if Mervyn loved *him*," Josephine had opined after Iris had read her part of a letter in which he had described Marco as looking like Donatello's David.

"I thought you didn't approve of assumptions."

"What do you mean?"

"Well, Marco is a ballet dancer."

"So?"

"And you know what people say about male ballet dancers."

"No, it's not that. You know I don't give a damn about that sort of thing. But Mervyn is one of God's gentle creatures, he's artistic... and Marco is artistic... he must be." She thought for a moment. "After all, why isn't he living with his family? They're from Melbourne. Why is he shacked up with Merv?"

"He's not shacked up, as you put it."

"You know what I mean. He's an impecunious student... he could be living at home for free... or in student accommodation."

"His family aren't happy about him being a ballet

dancer... they wanted him to be another Ron Barassi."

"How do you know? Has he any talent for Aussie Rules?"

"Something Mervyn said."

Marco did look like Donatello's David, as they had discovered later, on the first of many visits to them while he was continuing his training in London. Val had been at that idealistic age when young girls fall in love with male beauty and poets (the Rupert Brooke syndrome, Josephine called it) and Iris was thankful that he was as kind as he was handsome. Even Josephine had had to admit that while there was no denying the likeness, she thought it improbable that Mervyn would have been in love with him, or vice versa: "Too male-ish," she said.

Chapter 8

She sat up suddenly. Her heart was thumping. She hadn't been asleep, had she?

"Jo?" She thought she heard voices. "I must be dreaming. Jo, are you all right?" The muscles in her arms and shoulders ached. She got up from the bed as quickly as the stiffness would allow - every bit of her ached - and went along the landing. Josephine was talking to someone. Iris stopped. For a moment she wondered if Val had come home during the night, but Josephine was alone. Iris could hear the cadences of her speech without being able to distinguish more than a word here and there, as if it were a foreign language.

"Are you all right, Jo?"

"Oh, Iris, is that you? I've been dreaming. It must have been those photos. A right Pandora's Box you opened there."

"I thought I heard voices."

"No."

"How do you feel this morning?"

"I ache all over."

"Me too. Do you want a cup of tea?"

"Please."

Iris picked up Josephine's eiderdown from the newell post and took it back to her bedroom. "Anything you want while I'm here?" she called.

"No thanks."

On her way down the stairs she removed the plank and carried it to the kitchen.

"I've made some toast. We might as well have

some breakfast." She elbowed the duvet aside and put the tray down in the space beside Josephine.

"I had the weirdest dreams. It was most odd. My father and Albina and Ed all jumbled in together. It was that damned album. I suppose Ed's dead too by now."

"You didn't keep in touch with him?"

"No."

"Didn't you even write to him?"

"Nope."

"Did he write to you?"

"Once or twice."

"What did he say?"

"I didn't open them."

"Oh, Jo."

"You're far too sentimental, Iris."

Iris spread butter and marmalade on another slice of toast and handed it to her.

"And you run away from things."

"I have never run away from anything in my life."

"Not true."

"Even this nonsense about dying."

"Everyone has to die. I'm facing it,"

"You're going to be eighty, and there's plenty of life left in you. How about facing that?"

"What's brought this on all of a sudden?"

"All day yesterday and most of last night I was thinking about it one way or another."

"Well, just stop it." There was silence except for the munching of toast. "You've always had this thing about running away." Iris said nothing. "Well, perhaps you're right. People do run away. From all sorts of things, not just danger."

"Like those people in Piraeus."

"Yes. Like those people in Piraeus. From poverty."

"From unhappiness." Iris thought of Nick. "From all sorts of things."

Josephine sipped her tea. "Before I went to Australia, my father had a motor accident. Did I tell you?" Iris shook her head, Josephine knew perfectly well she hadn't told her. "Nothing serious, his car was hardly dented. But he'd a bit of a knock, and I thought he ought to have an X-ray just to be on the safe side." She revolved her mug slowly between her hands. "The X-rays were fine, all anyone was looking for were bony injuries and there weren't any." She drained the mug in one gulp. "What there *was*, was a tumour. In the pancreas. Not sufficiently advanced to give any symptoms but..." she enunciated each word softly and very precisely, "so far advanced that there was no point in mentioning it."

"Jo." Iris didn't know what to say.

"I didn't mention it, and he didn't, although I'm damned sure he saw it, he was too good a doctor not to. And I answered an advertisement for a post in Melbourne."

Iris heard the bracket clock chiming seven o'clock. She poured some more tea for both of them and they drank in silence.

"I think," she scrutinised the contents of her half-empty mug, "people only run away from themselves, really. Although I suppose if they knew that they wouldn't bother."

"I expect they would. They just wouldn't believe it."

Iris smiled at her. "And I think that's an oversimplification."

"Probably."

"Come on. It's time we were on the move."

Josephine put her plate and mug on the tray and Iris pushed it as far to one side as possible. No sense in making unnecessary journeys.

"Do you want to use the potty?"

Josephine made a face. "I'm going to have a go at making it to the bathroom. Keep it in reserve."

They discovered that it is extremely difficult for anyone, other than a toddler, to crawl up the stairs, and virtually impossible for anyone six feet tall and stiff in the joints, so once again Iris had to manhandle Josephine up one stair at a time and, in so doing, discovered too just which specific action related to which specific aching muscle. And how she ached! They stopped for a breather at the top of the stairs.

"Ba gum, Mum, ma bum's numb!" Obviously Josephine ached too. She rolled bumpily from one buttock to the other, rubbing as she rolled. "Oh boy!"

"I'm not surprised."

"I am old. I am old..."

"Come on."

"'I shall wear the bottoms of my trousers rolled.' I'm old, Iris, old, old, old, old."

"You're only a day older than yesterday. You didn't go on like this then."

"I wasn't old then."

"Well, you poor old thing, do you think you could manage to crawl to the loo now?" She saw the protest forming on Josephine's lips. "I know it's not very dignified," there was only a faint snort, "but you might get there quicker that way."

"I'm bloody stiff."

"Have a go."

Josephine set off, unwillingness manifest in every unsteady movement. She looked up at Iris. "You're lording it over me. Don't just stand there cracking your whip. I'm not some beast of burden." So, to encourage her, Iris got down on all fours as well, and they crawled along the passage together. At the bathroom door they over-reached themselves and collapsed, wedged side by side in the doorway, brawling like urchins. Iris began to laugh more and more hysterically. Soon they were both clinging to each other, helpless with laughter.

"Shut up, Iris, for God's sake, or I'll wet myself."

Iris was still giggling.

"Do you want the potty?"

"Hell, no!" She clenched her teeth, visibly willing her hands and knees to move across the bathroom carpet as quickly as they would go, until she reached her goal. She was gasping for breath. "You'll have to help me."

"Kneel up."

Josephine did as she was told. Iris clasped her round her middle and, with a huge amount of gasping and grunting from them both, managed unceremoniously to yank her bottom up into the air, holding her there before pulling down her pyjama trousers, lifting the lid and plonking her down on the lavatory in one triumphant movement.

"I can hear the telephone. Stay there."

"I won't move, I promise."

Unco-ordinatedly, Iris half slithered, half ran down the stairs into the sitting-room.

"Mother? Mum, are you ok? You sound out of breath. I didn't wake you up, did I?"

"No, no," Iris panted, "no, we've been up some time. We've had our breakfast. How about you?"

"I just thought I'd give you a ring before I start work. How is Jo? What sort of night did you have?"

"All right. Everything's fine. Jo slept well, she says, and…"

"How about you?"

"Darling, I'm fine. Really. You don't have to worry about a thing. You'll see when you get back. Thank you for ringing. I hope things go well today. Have you had a proper breakfast?"

"Yes, I have."

"Not just a cup of coffee?"

"Now, Mum, don't worry. It's not like 'A' Levels. Everything's under control. I've had a proper breakfast. I've even got time to do the washing up and housework before I have to leave!"

"No last minute swotting?"

"Mum! If I don't know it all by now, it's too damn late." She sounded like Josephine.

"No, no… you said… it's not 'A' Levels. Oh, it is good to hear you, darling. Thank you for ringing."

"Tell Jo I've got some news for her. For both of you. That should buck her up."

"Oh, lovely. What is it?"

"This evening. You'll have to wait. Eddie sends his love. Love to Jo. I must go. 'Bye now. God bless."

"Love to Edwin. God bless," she replaced the receiver slowly, "hurry back," and sat down in the window-seat.

Chapter 9

"She looks so tiny. How could they dress her in black like that?" Iris watched the child walking ahead of them with un-child-like composure towards the church. "What's going to become of her?"

"Ruth's parents," Josephine nodded towards the elderly couple who were accompanying the little girl, "or Bill and Catherine. There's going to be a family discussion about it after the service."

"We could have her." Iris held her breath, the words had popped out of her mouth before she had even had time to think them.

Josephine frowned. "Don't be silly, Iris."

"I'm not being silly."

"Bill's the better bet," Josephine went on as if nothing had been said, "I know Gerry would approve, there was only a year between them. After all, he's got kids already, he and Catherine won't even notice one more. And anyway, it'll be company for her," she looked towards the child, "help her get over all this."

"But Jo, they've got *four* children," more than their fair share, she had been tempted to say, "and they're all older than her. They may not want another one." They filed through the church doorway. "*And* two of each." She lowered her voice. "An extra girl, especially an only child who's been used to being the only one, mightn't fit in. Think of that. And we haven't anything... anyone... except us."

"A child needs a father."

"Well, she'd have two mothers instead." By now Iris had no doubts at all. And Josephine, she knew, was the very person you could persuade to do something on the spur of the moment. "You wouldn't have to worry about her. I could look after her. She's a dear little thing. And a good sport, you said so yourself. Please, Jo."

So engrossed was she by the possibilities in this new line of thought that the funeral service passed largely unnoticed save for an occasional glance at the dry-eyed child who was behaving so correctly that it was Iris whose eyes filled with tears, and only the thought of Josephine which prevented her from shedding them.

She had met Gerald and his handsome wife Ruth less than half a dozen times in the two years since she and Josephine had returned from Australia, and indeed felt that she hardly knew them at all, whereas their young daughter had been a frequent visitor to their house. She was not only an only child, but something of an afterthought as well, being the only child of middle-aged parents who already had a well-established, well-ordered, childless life (replete with business trips abroad, and numerous engagements in London) and who, with the birth of their daughter, saw no reason to alter anything. And now, suddenly, everything had been overturned by a car crash in fog on the new M4 motorway.

At the end of the service the arguments for and against continued on the short journey from the church to the hotel in Canterbury where Iris and Josephine had, in fact, spent the previous night. Private rooms had been reserved for luncheon and after the meal, when the family friends had dispersed, Iris was left to take the orphan into an adjoining sitting-room. They sat bolt upright in two armchairs facing each other.

"Is there anything you'd like to do? Would you like me to read to you?" Iris had brought a favourite book.

"No, thank you. I don't want anything, thank you."

She was so still, this wintry child dressed all in black, with her straight, dark hair and her pale face and her dark, straight eyebrows above anxious eyes. Iris longed to hug some warmth into her. She smiled with what assurance she could muster, and the child gave a faint smile in return. It would be a mistake to do anything too precipitately. The child got to her feet and moved over to Iris's chair and, without looking at her or saying a word, sat down beside her. Iris put an arm round her and suddenly there she was with her face pressed into Iris's shoulder and her whole body shaking. Iris stroked her hair and rocked her, murmuring comforting wordless sounds, until gradually the sobbing died down to a few intermittent gulps and Iris was able to fumble for the large cotton handkerchief she knew was in her handbag, and dry her eyes and her face and blow her nose. And so they sat, squeezed together, waiting to be summoned.

Bill came for them and, as they walked hand-in-hand through the doorway to the dining-room, Iris glanced towards Josephine who, annoyingly, was preoccupied with her diary and did not look up.

"Valentina, my dear," it was Ruth's father who spoke once they were seated, "we have been discussing your future home. But, before we decide finally, you must tell us what you think." Was that Josephine's idea? Iris wondered. "Now, my dear, I hope you know that you will always have a home with Granny and me. Your mother was our daughter…" he faltered, "and I know that she and your father… and … and we would be very happy for you to come and live with us, as you have been doing for these last few days, but we have to think of what's best for you. We are getting old and we are not sure whether it would be fair to you for you always to be with old people. Especially when you have aunts and uncles with children of their own," Iris's hopes sank, "who all want you to make your home with them." There was a general murmur of assent from all her aunts and uncles, and his wife, who was sitting next to him, smiled at him. He looked kindly at his youngest granddaughter and cleared his throat. "However, your aunt Josephine has suggested…" Iris didn't hear any more. She looked questioningly at Josephine, who grinned at her, and then tried desperately to make sense of what he was saying in case she had got it wrong, but she hadn't. "I suggest you try it for a little while," he was continuing, "and see what you think. It needn't be a final decision, you understand. See how you get on." Iris had stopped breathing altogether.

Valentina stood up. She looked at her grandparents and at her aunts and uncles - apparently it had not been considered suitable for any of her cousins to attend the funeral - her face was expressionless. She turned towards Iris and then looked across at Josephine.

"Thank you, Granny and Grandpa, I would like that."

Iris breathed again.

Chapter 10

There was no doubt that it had been a success from every point of view.

Josephine had always called her niece Val, Valentina being at once too much of a mouthful and much too fanciful, in her opinion; and since titles such as "aunt" or, worse, "auntie" were anathema to her she had always been plain Jo. Iris, in a whimsical moment, had suggested "Mother Iris" for herself to distinguish between her and the child's mother, but the teasing was so relentless that she contented herself with "Mother" - or "Mum" when Josephine wanted to annoy her. These days, though, Val nearly always called her "Mum" and she didn't mind one bit. She gave up her job, and with it relinquished any regrets and griefs from the past. And for the first time in her experience the household had settled into something like real contentment - even Josephine had seemed to grow more settled, not that she became in any way domesticated, but gone was that unsettling passion for change. To be sure, the expeditions to some of the more exotic parts of the world were still undertaken every three or four years, and when her niece was old enough she often accompanied her aunt, and showed, according to that zestful traveller, all the relish for discomfort combined with an ability to adapt and invent that were prerequisites in a truly congenial travelling companion. But the desire to tear up her life by its roots had, as far as Iris could tell, become less and less insistent. Whether this was due to increase of years (Josephine would never have admitted as much and certainly, physically, she had seemed ageless for so long that her announcement of a few days ago had found Iris totally unprepared) or to the fact that she had acquired a family of her own, was impossible to say. But, whatever the reason, as her eightieth birthday approached, she had acknowledged that she was unlikely to move very far any more.

Yet still that one last journey, the epic journey which they had talked about and planned and played with for years like some rainy day pastime, was there waiting. It was a journey which would take them all (for Iris, too, was to be of the party) overland to Petra by camel (she wasn't quite sure about that) and on to Pakistan and India, then east by way of Bangladesh and the country Iris still thought of as Burma and so on down through Malaysia until they ended up in Singapore. "We'll celebrate with a gin-sling at Raffles," Josephine had promised, "and after that I'll hang up my binoculars and take up knitting."

Unlike most of her projects, this one had, so far at any rate, failed to materialise, and now Iris supposed that it never would, although with the passing years it had become so much a part of their collective thinking that, in moments of absentmindedness, she sometimes forgot that it hadn't actually taken place. The germ of the idea had, in a way, been hers, for when Josephine had made it absolutely clear that she intended to leave Australia for good, Iris had suggested that they might drive back to England along a similar route, but in reverse. However, Josephine had - rather uncharacteristically, Iris thought - dismissed the whole thing as being far too circuitous for their requirements. She wished to get home by the fastest route possible. "You'd have thought all the devils in hell were after her!" Iris had observed to Mervyn. "Talk about fleeing the country!" And so the epic journey had been discussed and plotted and dreamed about and shelved, and dusted off from time to time to be inspected afresh, until Iris accepted that it would never happen. "I don't even mind particularly. And it's not just the camels!" She would have liked to have seen the Taj Mahal, of course she would, and all the other places, but might they not have turned out to be less beautiful than in imagination? And besides, she knew that the Taj Mahal was incomplete and that there ought to have been a black mirror-image to complement it. The reality, no matter how beautiful, might have been a disappointment. She kept such fancies to herself.

The child would have two mothers. Hadn't Juno said that in 'Juno and the Paycock'? When Iris said it she had had little or no idea, beyond intuition, of just how those two mothers would balance each other. Where Iris was gentle, Josephine was stimulating and full of plans for outings and activities, deriding Iris's protectiveness and caution with good-humoured scorn. If Val wanted stilts or roller-skates she would have them, if she wanted a bicycle then a bicycle she would have, rather than the tricycle Iris favoured. And when Val wanted to study medicine, Iris's suggestion that perhaps physiotherapy or nursing might be more suitable had been vigorously refuted. And Valentina had, in her own way, balanced both her mothers, being at once compliant and adventurous, affectionate and unsentimental and, mercifully, since Josephine could not possibly have tolerated a stupid child, intelligent. "She's a better doctor than me," Josephine had said in a rare moment of self-awareness, and over-riding Iris's loyal protests, "her intelligence is informed by love." Now, she and her Australian friend, Edwin Murray, were both sitting the Membership examination and, if she passed - which neither Josephine nor Iris had the least doubt about - she would be a physician; and Josephine, for all her disparagement of any doctor except her father and her colleagues in the Flying Doctor Service and, possibly, her partner, John, was intensely proud of her.

Heavens above! Iris shook herself out of her daydream. If she didn't get a move on, Val would have finished her exam and arrived home and Josephine would still be sitting on the loo! She stood up. Climbing the stairs required considerably more of an effort than it had done yesterday, and there was still quite a way to go. She tried to put it out of her mind.

Josephine was indeed still sitting on the loo. Iris felt surprised that she hadn't called out but all she said was: "I can't go on, Iris. I can't go any further. It's no use. You'll just have to leave me here till Val gets back."

"You can't go on?" Her voice came out in a hiss. "You can't go on?" The hiss crescendoed to a screech. "I have pushed and pulled and... lugged you up all those *BLOODY STAIRS*," Josephine looked startled, "and you crumple up and say you can't go on? You'll go on if it *kills* you! If it kills *me*!! Now, get up. At once! Get on your feet!" She seized her by the shoulders and shook her so fiercely that Josephine's face turned crimson with astonishment. Iris was pretty astonished herself. It was amazing that she didn't rattle.

"Yes, Iris." And with some panting and puffing, Josephine levered herself up off the seat. Her pyjama trousers slithered to the floor in a heap and Iris laughed, once again on the edge of hysteria, and bent down to retrieve them. "Come on, you great lummox."

After a few false starts, they evolved a reasonably successful and rather more dignified method of travel, with Iris walking backwards holding Josephine's hands firmly in hers, like a human Zimmer frame. She hoped that Josephine couldn't read her thoughts.

"What bugs me is these piddling little steps. Why can't I move properly like I used to? The legs just won't go."

Physiotherapy, my girl, that's what you need, Iris decided, and decided also that she would leave it to Val to suggest it.

"Val says she has some news for us."

"Did she say what?"

"No."

"Not even a hint?"

"Not even a hint."

"Then I wish you hadn't told me."

They needed a diversion. "Tell me about Ed."

"Ed?"

"Ed Murray, wasn't it?"

"I've already told you about him."

"Not why you didn't marry him, you haven't."

"I married you instead."

"Fool!"

Josephine threw back her head and laughed. Iris had seen her once across the lounge on board the S.S. Himalaya, surrounded by young officers, and she had thrown back her head then and laughed in just the same way and they had laughed with her. That time it had been anger which had dissolved, now it was fatigue.

"I've always deplored the assumptions men make."

"I beg your pardon?"

"I've always called the shots, you know that, but with Ed... for the first time in my life... for the only time... I was happy to be..." they shuffled slowly along together in silence and, not for the first time in their journeyings, Iris wondered whether perhaps Josephine had given up on the idea of speech, until she spat out the single word "subservient." She stopped and drew herself up to her full height. "I watched myself being subservient and..." she fixed Iris with a glare, "and revelling in it, and I hated myself. Drooling over some man like a love-sick schoolgirl. It was disgusting. Mooning about in a daze of misery if he didn't phone. God!"

"So, why didn't you..?"

Josephine laughed, a quiet, unamused laugh. "He whistled for me."

Iris didn't understand.

"To go with him. Like you would a dog."

Iris doubted it.

"And I jumped up just as if he'd said 'walkies!' You want to know why I went scurrying back to Melbourne with my tail between my legs? That was why. Some man in the outback who'd never read a book in his life whistled for me. *Me!*"

"You haven't read that many books yourself."

"You know what I mean."

"I wish you'd told me."

"There was no point."

"It was a joke."

"No."

"It must have been, surely?"

Josephine laughed again, and this time there was wry amusement in it. "He didn't even know he was doing it."

"He looks so nice in his photos."

"He *was* nice. A great bloke." She started to move again. "Good," she shuffled forward a step, "honest," another shuffle, "kind," and another while she added to the catalogue, "uncomplicated. It would have been a disaster."

Iris nodded. "Just as well he whistled then."

"Hmph."

The conversation, punctuated as it had been by halts for breath or halts for thought, had lasted several minutes; in all it must have taken them nearly half an hour to get from the bathroom to the bedroom door. Josephine leaned against the doorway.

"Don't stop now."

"Just for a moment."

Iris had an inspiration: "You know that photo?"

"Which photo?"

"The one of the garden. It's just come to me. It was Albina's garden... the one she made. You remember. At the very end of their garden... that little secluded bit?" Josephine shook her head. "I saw her in there once, not long before..." she broke off. Michael must have carried her there, she was too ill to move by then. "Of course. I remember. She made it when her mother died. A sort of memorial, I suppose. She went to no end of trouble to get it right. She did a lot of the work herself, don't you remember? She had a thing about everything looking weathered, as if it had always been there. She used to ask your advice."

"I never saw it."

"Yes, you did. She used to sit in it when she was ill." Now, looking back, it seemed almost as if she had created it for that very purpose.

"No."

"You carried her there yourself once. You told me."

"I don't remember. Nope." Josephine was emphatic.

"I know who took the picture. Mervyn." Iris was triumphant.

"Mervyn never saw it."

"Yes, he did. He must've done. Surely you remember? They postponed little Josephine's christening because Albina's mother had died... they didn't have it till about a year later. He was one of the godparents... with you. He came over for it. You must remember. He was rather a good photographer. It was quite a hobby of his."

"No. Don't remember anything about it."

Won't remember, more like! But Iris was concerned at how breathless Josephine was becoming, and said nothing. Lightly she suggested: "Now... how about a hop, skip and a jump to your bed?"

"Don't joke, love."

"Come on, you can make it. Take a little run at it."

Josephine launched her tall frame at the bed, but her feet failed to keep up with her and she crashed to her knees beside it, gasping for breath.

"*Jo!*" Iris was furious. "What did you want to do

that for?"

"Well, you said 'take a run at it.'"

"Yes, well... I never thought you'd take it literally. You'd better say a quick prayer for both of us while you're down there. Come on, I'll help you up."

"Say a quick prayer yourself! You're too bloody cheerful by half." Her eyes closed wearily. "I don't want to remember Albina like that," she was talking to herself, her voice barely audible, "I want to remember her as she was." She looked up at Iris. "*That* wasn't Albina."

Iris bent and planted a kiss on the top of her head.

"What on earth did you do that for?"

"To encourage you."

"Don't be so damn cheerful."

Iris did not feel particularly cheerful.

"What's this?" Josephine fished a sagging, baggy, cold, hot water bottle from the bed.

"Good Lord, I'd forgotten that. I'll do you another."

"Don't bother. Just give me a leg up." Iris obliged, and in a surprisingly short time Josephine was lying back against the pillows, pink in the face and panting heavily. "God, that's good." Iris plumped up the pillows round her and tidied the bedclothes. "You're a brick."

"Let's have some coffee."

"Not just now. Sit down for a bit."

Iris flopped into the armchair by the window and leaned against the bedspread folded over the back of it. It was yesterday when she had made it all ready. Yesterday. It seemed like a week ago. "I'm sorry I rattled you like that."

"It doesn't matter."

"It does though. I hope I didn't hurt you."

Josephine shook her head.

"Anyway, I'm sorry." She started to get up but Josephine waved her back into the chair. "If I stay sitting down I'll never get up again."

"It doesn't matter."

"It does. I've a heap of things I ought to be doing."

"What, for instance?"

"The washing up. Making something for tonight. I ought to pop out and do a bit of shopping." She hadn't even had a chance to wash her face or anything.

"Leave it. You have just accomplished something bloody marvellous. Sit down and do nothing for a few minutes." She closed her eyes. "I never thought we'd make it, you know."

"I tried not to think about it."

"And when we got to the landing... that was brilliant. Inspired."

"What was? What are you talking about?" Josephine seemed to be losing her grip on things.

"Leaving me there for the night."

"Really? Why?"

"Psychologically. It was the time when most travellers do something stupid."

"I don't really see what else we could have done."

"I left the glider once to go for help, something you're told never to do." Iris wondered whether she had missed part of the narrative. "I'd run out of thermals, and I was stuck out in the bush somewhere... completely lost... and I thought I knew better. I was lucky not to die out there."

"Get some rest, love, you're tired."

"And you're humouring me. I know what I mean."

She knew what she meant
There had been times back in the wing chair when she had seen things so clearly that even the memory of it dazzled her - only now she could not quite remember what it had all been about. Iris said that she had said she was dying, and that she proposed to die there, with her boots on. Well, Iris was truthful as a rule. No. She was always truthful, even when you didn't want her to be, like that business with Albina's father. Here she, Josephine, was dying, and Iris didn't pull her punches even now. So Iris must be right. But she had come so far along the road since then that the beginning of the journey was lost and no longer mattered.

"Have you enjoyed your life, Iris?"

In the belief that Josephine was asleep, Iris had relaxed, letting her mind wallow in the luxury of not thinking at all. For the past twenty-four hours it had been like Waterloo Station in the rush-hour in there, and now the total absence of thought made her feel as if she was floating. It was with the greatest difficulty that she brought herself down to where the question waited. Had she enjoyed her life?

"I think so."

"Unequivocally?"

"Unequivocally? Yes. Looking back on it as a whole, the answer must be 'yes'. Even the bad bits. And you know? I think how surprised my mother," she glanced heavenwards, "must be when she sees how my life has turned out. I'm sorry to say it pleases me."

"You were far too good for your mother."

"No, not too good." She shook her head. "Just the wrong daughter for her. Rose was more what she wanted, I suppose. At least she had her to be proud of. One out of two isn't bad, is it? Why?"

"Oh... just wandering... wondering."

"How about you?"

"The same. I'd like it to go on a bit longer... one more journey..."

There was a journey once... once... her travelling companion shadowy, always hooded... and silent... although not uncongenial. Horses' hooves - horses, she had noted, not camels - horses' hooves stirring the dust of deserts, day after timeless day, with the chink, chink of metal and jingling of little bells edging the softly creaking harnesses the only sounds as they followed an invisible trail as surely as predestination.

"Show me your face."

Her companion rode on in silence. She spurred her horse to catch up. "Show me."

On this journey they had had no need of water, which seemed strange now that she thought about it, neither had their horses, nor any need of food.

"All my life I have feared you. Not for myself, but then you know that. You have been my adversary. I only begrudged you one victory. And now we travel together. I should like to see your face."

"In good time."

"Iris?"

"Yes?"

"Have you enjoyed your life?"

"Try to get some rest. Val will be here later. She has something special to tell us."

"She's going to marry that doctor of hers."

"How do you know?"

"I know. They'll both get their Memberships, and he'll take her back to Australia."

"You're very certain."

"Yes, I am. What will you do?"

"Stay here with you?"

"Ah."

White rooms have a special stillness all their own, Iris thought.

"I couldn't forgive her, you know."

"Who?"

"Albina. She was against me. I thought we were fighting it together and all the time she was against me. *She was on your side.*"

"My side? What do you mean, my side?"

"No, not yours. *Yours. Well, you're not winning this time. Not yet.*"

Silence again.

"We could go with them."

"What, all the way to Australia?"

"Why not? Not with them all the time, of course, but overland some of the way. Do the journey we've never done."

"I thought you said you were dying?"

"I've changed my mind."